I0682742

LAND
of
LYONESSE

BOOK THREE OF THE *LAND TRILOGY*

PEGGY GARDNER

Land of Lyonesse
Copyright © 2016 Peggy C. Gardner

ALL RIGHTS RESERVED. No part of this book may be reproduced or transmitted in any form or by any means, electronic or mechanical, including photocopying, recording, or by any information storage and retrieval system, without permission in writing from the publisher.

This book is a work of fiction. All names, characters, places, and incidents in the book are products of the author's imagination, used fictitiously, and not to be construed as actual. Any resemblance to real events, locales, organizations, or people—living or dead—is coincidental.

ISBN: 978-1-944878-22-1

For my children, Morgan and Nick, and my nieces and nephews who have listened to my stories for many years.

Charleston, Oregon

Hal Hatchet: After my identical twin James eloped with my fiancée Clara seventeen years ago, I removed the word "regret" from my lexicon. Yesterday, I was broadsided by regret when the mirror image of my long-dead mother wearing a mini skirt came strutting down the boardwalk at the Charleston marina and passed out at my feet.

I had never seen my fifteen-year-old niece, Jenny Hatchet, nor did I know that my twin brother had died over a year ago driving a truck into the McKenzie River. My shock when a teenage girl collapsed at my feet couldn't compare to the thunderbolt that struck Jenny who thought she was seeing her father back from the grave.

The fickleness of her mother Clara—who had unknowingly married a polygamist two months ago and taken both of her daughters off to a remote compound in Idaho—didn't surprise me in the least. Jenny had escaped from the perverts to a nearby Native American reservation, but Clara and her younger daughter remained as captives in the compound.

This beautiful, bright, but resentful niece of mine appeared out of nowhere with two boys, Heathcliff and Hareton, from the family who had sheltered her on the nearby reservation. So, in a state of disbelief about what had happened to my brother's family, I tried to make amends to Jenny. I guess I didn't try hard enough. I should have instantly called out the National Guard or taken my rifle and laid siege to the polygamy compound.

After the happiest day I can remember in years of being on the river and crabbing with my niece and her two friends, they disappeared. The boys had been ecstatic about my plans for an ocean fishing trip the next day. When I left to gas up the boat, I returned to find them gone and a perfunctory thank-you note from Jenny.

The brevity, terseness, and underlying criticism in her note cut me to the quick:

"Dear Uncle Hal, Thank you for your hospitality. I will manage to rescue Mother and Lorena without your help. Have a nice life catching fish. Jenny."

CHAPTER 1

Stuffed into a coffin-shaped box in Jerry Winner's van, the only part of my stiffening carcass still functioning was my brain.

When Jerry's crusty thumbs circled my neck today in that alley in Spokane, I could feel him palpating my sternocleidomastoid muscle, searching for the dead giveaway of a throbbing fountain near the fourth cervical vertebra.

Bingo. Contact. Blackness. I would go to my grave with an image of Munch's screamer imprinted on my retinas. The scream came from the gaping mouth of Maylene Darken, one of the two stepmothers that my mother's bigamist husband, Gomer Obadiah Darken, had foisted off on me.

When Heathcliff Earnshaw, his younger brother Hareton, and I stopped by the Farmers Market in Spokane—after our pointless trip to the Oregon Coast to find my missing uncle and get his help—I had lured Maylene into an alley for a chinwag about the status of my mother and little sister.

Like a candy-ass, I'd left my mother and sister Lorena behind when I escaped from the Compound of Perversion, better known as the Church of the Protectors of Restored Christianity in Northern Idaho.

Minutes ago, death had paid me a visit via Jerry's thumbs. Of that I was certain. Ever since the sudden death of my father, who veered his truck into the McKenzie River, I sensed that the old hooded spook with the scythe was just waiting for the right moment to whack me.

Flat on my back in a makeshift casket, I could feel every bump in the road. The disgusting odor of lye infused with thyme let me know that the bulges alongside my neck were bars of unsold soap from the Farmers Market. I was sharing my coffin with leftover "organic" products that rankled with pesticides and chemicals.

All that postmortem speculation about lights at the end of the tunnel could be put to rest. I could feel an opaque glaze gelling under my closed lids. Organs with no oxygen did whatever they did with no more bodily functions to support. They went flaccid as an old dishrag.

The soup making of putrefaction must already be underway in my body—all those anaerobic organisms proliferating faster than Sherman marched through Atlanta. Give me three to six hours, and my limbs would be as rigid as flagpoles. Another few hours and bloat from methane would turn me into a puffer fish.

Without an undertaker's palette of makeup, my face would discolor into a bluish-purple that wouldn't go well with my chestnut hair. Vanity seemed to be traveling into the grave with me.

It's probably not a light at the end of the tunnel that the newly revived recall; it's most likely the victim's last cognizant struggle to preserve the brain against microbes fighting their way up to the big valve, the one where Jerry put his odious thumb.

I tried to remember the Bouthillier nomenclature but

couldn't get past cervical, petrous, and lacerum as I worked my way mentally up the vertebrae of my neck, wondering where the blood stopped pumping.

When the old van chugged through the Compound gates, I could envision the reception my corpse would get. Jerry Winner and his partner in crime, Enoch Bonner, might bear me through the gates on their shoulders like the fallen queen Boudicca who chose death over captivity.

Or, they might not. They might just plop me into that murky pond where Jerry dumped my friend Abigail Johnson.

Dismal thoughts shouldn't torment the last moments of the dead, but I was in mental throes over being dumped into water more than six inches deep. Can't swim. Even a bathtub of water sends my blood pressure soaring.

If those Uzi-toting elders let the van into the Compound, I reflected, with a tinge of satisfaction, that some of the CPRCers might regret their treatment of me, especially after I'd rewired their soap factory and chapel.

I may have descended into blindness, but I could still imagine Mother and my little sister wailing over my limp body; I visualized their future. Mother would sink into a Valium fog. Lorena would be tutored in obedience until one of those Abraham-demented men decided a thirteen-year-old nubile girl was age-appropriate for the sacrificial altar of a "celestial marriage."

Maybe a marriage with our own stepfather, Gomer Darken. I had watched him holding Lorena on his lap, nuzzling her tousled golden locks like a hog rooting for truffles, smirking at Mother as though he had just found Lolita.

The van hit a big pothole, jarring my backbone like a

string of off-centered dominoes. I had a sudden vision of myself as Lazarus from a Fifteenth Century Byzantine icon, standing with a halo glinting around my head while peasants picked at my mummy wrappings.

I stirred. From my dead toes to somewhere in the recesses of my tortured brain, things were moving. From beyond the veil—or whatever dark place I had gone—I squeezed my eyes open just a slit to see a tunnel of light. It was coming through a very dirty back window of Jerry's van.

At that moment, Emily Dickinson breathed her poem about hope into my deaf ears.

Hope is the thing with feathers
That perches in the soul
And sings the tune
Without the words
and never stops at all.

I flung myself into an upright position so quickly that my head gyrated, scrambling the light like a lopsided kaleidoscope. Pottery plates flew in all directions; bars of Sion soap skidded across the ridged metal floor, and I stared into the shocked faces of three women sitting on wooden benches along the side of the van as though they were being transported to lockdown.

The llama face of Marybeth Darken, stepmother number two, looked primed for a good spit. Maylene, stepmother number one, had the grace to utter words that the other two women would never speak: "Praise the Lord. She's restored."

*And with all her wits about h*er I wanted to scream to high heaven into those disbelieving faces.

CHAPTER 2

The moment I was fully conscious, my wits went into high gear. When captured by perverts, the captive must practice perversion as a fine defensive art. I would start with those two bullies in the front seat.

Jerry struggled to keep the van from swerving as he watched me rising into his rearview mirror like Venus on her clamshell. My butt-clinging skirt covered a bit more than the locks of Venus.

I ignored Jerry and smiled warmly into Enoch's slack-jawed face. "I've missed seeing you, Enoch. The Winner family refused to let you visit me in their attic jail no matter how often I asked."

All the "well I nevers" popping out from between Leah Winner's jaws provided perfect background music for my circus tricks.

During the two weeks I spent with the Earnshaw family on the Reservation after escaping from the Compound, I learned that when Elder Winner and Elder Bonner had taken over a few years earlier, rules had changed. Multiple wives and subjugation of females had become common practice.

Glazed with the ice of revulsion, I had repulsed advances by the two elders' sons, Jerry and Enoch. A week before I escaped the Compound, I had been trussed turkey-fashion by the elders and left in the Winner attic until my animosity toward Jerry could cool into compliance. I would then submit to a celestial union in their chapel.

As I festered in the attic like Rochester's mad wife, I knew beyond a doubt that Jerry would strangle me as he had his fiancée Abigail Johnson, disguising her murder as suicide by drowning. My meek friend Abigail never gave him cause. I did. Every time he opened my door, I lashed him with more tongues than Cerberus.

I knew it would be only a matter of time before I pushed Jerry over the edge—or he shoved me out the attic window—my unholy fear of water above my knees wouldn't make suicide by drowning plausible.

As the van bounced along the highway with me sitting upright in the wooden box, I grinned over at the third wife of Elder Winner. Leah had been too dim-witted to spot the tools of a jailbreak. She had even helped my stepmother Maylene carry an aspidistra plant up the stairs without noticing that it was housed in a macramé sheath made with 40 feet of paracord.

I knew that the mother of Josh Barnes—a boy with more dimples than Jude Law and better abs than Matthew McConaughey—had provided the means for my escape with the paracord and a knife buried in the soil of the aspidistra. Maylene had delivered the plant to my attic room, probably unaware of what she was bringing.

Or, perhaps she was. There might be a bit more to

Maylene than her versifying. Today, she had seemed gen-
uinely happy to see me. Now, wedged along the side of the
van between her sisterwife, Marybeth, and Leah Winner,
Maylene appeared to be depressed. Or guilty. She should
be. She had spotted Jerry and Enoch in the alley just before
Jerry grabbed me.

However, I did remembered that she had baked me a
mile-high angel food cake for my birthday that first night
we arrived at the Honeymoon Retreat in the Compound
before we learned that Mother was bride number three for
Mr. Darken—and his first two, Maylene and Marybeth,
were still part of the happy family.

I flexed my feet against the end of what I thought of
as my coffin and an uneasy thought struck me. I might
have been Mr. Darken's fourth bride had it not been for
my irrepressible wit—aimed like a well-honed saber at him
and constant as the drip of water torture.

Before my stepfather made a deal with Elder Winner to
fob me off as a fiancée replacement, Jerry's sidekick Enoch
thought he would be the catch of the day.

From the minute Enoch planted his boot on my solar
plexus, after tripping me the morning of my first exploratory
run through the Compound, I could smell the pungent
odor of testosterone. As a peace offering, he had delivered
a wreath of dead quail to the front door with the panache
of a prom king toting an orchid wristlet.

My escape to the nearby Reservation appeared to have
healed the breach I had caused between Jerry and Enoch.
Jerry was the strangler in the alley, but it was Enoch's
goofy grin under his "King of Farts" baseball cap that I

PEGGY GARDNER

remembered just before the lights went out.

Better work on Enoch. I could still remember waking up in that attic to find Jerry surreptitiously squeezing my breasts like a sly shopper on the fruit aisle. "Copping any feels with sleeping girls these days, Jerry?"

Jerry steered wildly and flung an arm in my direction. I swerved with a lightening dodge, a move I had perfected around Jerry while I was captive in his family's attic.

Jerry's greased slab of nondescript brown hair and Hitler mustache reminded me so much of his idol, Adolph, that I almost favored that knuckle-headed Enoch—although a gas chamber had it hands down over the company of these two cretins.

An image of Scarlett O'Hara flirting outrageously with the Tarleton twins at the picnic on the cusp of the Civil War flashed before me. Her aim was to make Ashley Wilkes jealous. Mine was to set Jerry and Enoch at each other like pit bulls. If Josh Barnes felt even a frisson of jealousy, all the better.

"Actually," I drug out the word like a Southern belle, "I missed both of you during my little vacation on the Reservation. However, Heathcliff Earnshaw does know how to show a girl a good time."

Two of the sisterwives eyed me with undisguised curiosity, probably never having experienced a good time. Before I could think of another cheeky comment, Marybeth beat me to the punch.

"Good time cohabiting with savages, I reckon. That skirt would be a disgrace on a child the size of Lorena," Marybeth sniggered.

"Who named you head of the fashion police, Marybeth?" I snarled at her as Maylene slowly rotated her head as though to fend off my next barrage.

She was right. I needed to follow my clever instincts. Divide and conquer. Become like the worm in the apple—it hitches a ride inside the fruit and eats away unnoticed.

During those weeks at the Darken house when I had nothing else to read, I read in the Bible that James says we should bridle our tongues. I would try, but not with Marybeth. Civility was not possible. This woman had switched welts across my sister's legs for simply bringing her kitten into the house. I dipped my head to acknowledge Maylene's warning glance, all the while envisioning Marybeth's head, blackening on a pole just outside the Compound gates. Revenge in the Middle Ages had a certain pizzazz that I found very appealing when I looked at Marybeth.

Too light-headed to trust myself to flirt convincingly with Enoch and Jerry, I sank back into my coffin—the large wooden crate used for transporting bread, soap, pottery, pies and whatever the wives of the saints think the townspeople might buy at the Farmers Market.

As though my situation wasn't depressing enough, I had to bring up Heath. Funny, flirty Heathcliff Earnshaw—often on the edge of getting inside of my head to places I didn't want anyone to go.

The oldest Earnshaw son could have posed for a GQ cover; he often wore that smug look that comes with the self-assurance of fame. Aunt Izzy could always take him down a notch. She told me to call her Aunt Izzy, so I could pretend to be her niece and keep a low profile on the Res—then she became the beloved aunt I'd never had.

Aunt Izzy had taken me into her home when Josh Barnes found me ill and unconscious in the forest after my escape. Josh had taken me to the Earnshaw's house on the Reservation.

Just as the van jolted me back into the present, a nagging headache probed around in my left cerebral hemisphere—reserved strictly for my friend Euclid. Geometry was my passion, the only way for me to size up the world and have it make sense.

A sigh like a deflated balloon escaped from me. Considering the distance from Spokane to the Compound, surely no more than an hour had passed since Jerry and Enoch hauled me senseless into the van.

At this moment, I longed to be back with the Earnshaw family: Bill, the archeologist father who called me one "of his kids"; Hareton, a thirteen-year-old math whiz who idolized Euclid as much as I did; and, Cathy, a nine-year-old, who reminded me so much of Lorena that I happily overlooked her peevish nature.

I sat up quickly and gasped. "How far are we from Spokane? I need to let . . ."

"Let those people on the Res know you ain't coming back? You've done abusing their hospitality just like you abused Leah's."

The self-righteous look that Leah cast Marybeth told me that I had struck a nerve by cutting Leah's down comforter in half for a makeshift sleeping bag when I made my escape into the forest.

I put on my best woebegone face and turned it full force

on Leah Winner, Elder Winner's third wife, considerably far down in the pecking order of sisterwives.

"I feel terrible about your beautiful comforter. I shudder to think of all your work picking the down feathers off your geese."

The frozen expression on Leah's moon-shaped face matched the tension in my locked gut when I thought of those poor geese, clutched between her fat thighs as she ripped down off their breasts and sent them waddling off to grow another thatch.

"The idea of freezing in the forest made me desperate, Leah. So, I just took part of the comforter. Left half behind," I added as a partial apology.

"We will get to the bottom of this, Missy. Someone gave you an *implement*." Leah's head popped up from her thick neck, hissing like a cobra emerging from its basket. "You never could tear that comforter in half with only your hands."

"God gave me the implements," I said sweetly to her, flashing a toothy grin. "Not a cavity in them."

Maylene nodded with faintly disguised approval. I wasn't sure whether she was commending my dental hygiene or my deviousness. I needed to deflect attention away from Mrs. Barnes and Maylene—either one of them might have buried the knife in the roots of the aspidistra plant.

Josh's mother had troubles enough of her own. After sneaking into the Compound one night, hoping to see his best friend Josh, Heathcliff had met with Josh's mother and returned to the Res in frustration.

Heath had told Aunt Izzy that Josh's pickup was on blocks, and he was locked up at night in the single men's bunkhouse. Even more shocking, Josh's mother had been directed by the elders to give herself in celestial marriage to the sickly old Elder Grund, along with all her worldly goods.

A year before, Josh's father, the CPA for both the Compound and the Tribal organization, had been found gored to death by a dairy bull. Before calling the police, the elders had moved the body, cleaned up the pen, and hauled off the bull that Josh had speared with a hay fork when he discovered his dead father.

No one seemed inclined to question what an accountant was doing in a bullpen or why he had so conveniently faced an angry bull just before his family were preparing to leave the Compound forever. Josh had questions that he dared not voice. I was sure of that, especially since he had warned me about making imprudent comments around the elders.

CHAPTER 3

Closing my eyes, I propped my neck on the edge of the box and tried to think through the pain in my head. So many bad things had happened since Mother put Mr. Darken's two-caret ring on her finger back in Portland. Even after I escaped the Compound and found safety on the Reservation, disaster struck those around me.

Not Pip, I thought with a vague sense of relief. I had saved the wolfdog pup caught in an old spring-loaded trap in the forest. Dogs are resilient. Teenage girls aren't.

Less than a week ago, I had come upon the lifeless form of the dancing princess in the forest. On an early morning run, Heath and I had found his childhood friend's body. Someone had purposefully run over Sue Ann Snelling—and that tiny little creature in her womb. I didn't like to think of that. At least, the fetus wasn't Heath's.

To give us a breather from the suspicions and pain surrounding Sue Ann's murder—although they'd never put it that way—the Earnshaws had arranged a trip for Heath, Hareton and me to the south coast of Oregon. There, I was supposed find my father's brother, my Uncle Hal, a man I didn't know existed until Mother let it slip at my father's funeral.

Other than nice scenery and a look-see at my only uncle, the trip had been a bust. I had humiliated myself by fainting dead away on a boardwalk in Charleston. Mother neglected to mention that my uncle was an identical twin to my father.

After scooping up a relative he probably never wanted to see, the fisherman/sailor/long-lost uncle got to watch his niece in a heightened state of seasickness. Uncle Hal didn't offer to help rescue Mother and Lorena. And, I wasn't about to ask. He'd had over sixteen years to hold a grudge against my father for stealing his fiancée. Uncle Hal needed to get over it.

During our brief visit, Heath and Hareton achieved a fine level of camaraderie with Uncle Hal, mastering crabbing and boat navigation quickly. So, the minute Uncle Hal went on an errand, I made the boys skedaddle out of his house. No fond farewells for the uncle who had ignored my existence for fifteen years.

We were almost at the end of our trip back to the Reservation when we circled the Farmer's Market in Spokane. I had spotted the CPRC booth with its tatty "Organic and Safe" sign, but didn't say a word to Heath and Hareton.

Lord Nelson scenting victory at the Battle of Trafalgar while courting his own doom had nothing on me. Ditching the boys so that I could quiz Maylene alone, I had walked right into a trap.

Now, scrunched up against the sides of the box in the back of Jerry's van, I knew I looked exactly like the Delphic Sibyl in the Sistine Chapel, her fearful eyes cast askance at everyone looking in her direction.

Like the Sibyl, I knew who had done what, who was preparing to do even worse things, and I had no power to do anything but await fate. Or think and plot.

Uncle Hal might hold a grudge against my mother and father for falling in love and sailing away for a year and a day like the owl and the pussycat.

With identical twins lusting after her, Mother made the only wise decision of her life—the mathematician over the sailor. She should have said sorry to Uncle Hal, but Mother isn't skilled in linking action to consequence.

Uncle Hal and I shared the grudge-holding family gene. Resentment was my specialty, along with being able to cite all of Euclid's propositions, postulates, definitions and common notions flawlessly.

Eliminating Maylene as an unknown quantity, I peeked around the van at the cabal of four: Adolph and Knucklehead in the front seat and Marybeth and Leah on their bench, all watching me.

Celestial marriage kneaded the ids of Jerry and Enoch. Marybeth and Leah were bent on revamping me into a version of their dowdy selves. Stretched out in this makeshift bed, I was reminded of that Seventeenth Century doctor who carried a bat hidden in a pouch so that he could slit open the side of a patient, release the bat, and proclaim: "The devil has flown!"

Marybeth would be overjoyed to see the devil that she knew lodged inside of me. I wasn't sure about Leah Winner, but a triumphant grin spread across Jerry's face as the van chugged up the last hill toward the Compound's electrified fence.

Euclid's common notion came to me like a bolt: "Things which equal the same thing also equal one another." Scratch any one of these four fanatics in the van and depravity would ooze out. I locked my arms tight against me so it wouldn't splash on me.

SOMEONE MUST HAVE alerted the Compound. Mother, Lorena and Mr. Darken formed a jolly reception trio as the guards lowered their Uzis to let us in the gate.

Mother, Lorena and I clung to each other, weeping in relief like Titanic survivors. Mr. Darken looked on like a self-congratulatory captain who had steered around the iceberg.

A small group of CPRC onlookers watched our reunion with neutral faces as Marybeth crept inexorably around us, her snail horns twitching, checking for a weak spot. She found it.

My seven-year-old fashionista sister, Lorena, seemed more fixated on my clothes than my return and piped out: "Cool shirt, Jenny. I love the skull with sparkles for eye sockets and that glittery cross. Can I wear it?"

"Not unless you want to get to hell faster than you're headed at this minute." Marybeth gripped Lorena's arm, twisted it behind her back until she screamed in pain and shoved her toward Mrs. Johnson, the mother of my dead friend. Just before I escaped from the Compound, Lorena had been sent to live with the Johnsons for "acclimation."

For Lorena, that involved learning a new cosmology—angels, men, women and lesser beasts all stacked in a neat order on a world that might be flat. As for fashion, that meant bulbous floral skirts down to her ankles.

Acclimation shouldn't mean corporeal punishment of a child inflicted by her wicked stepmother. It wasn't just her mind that was out of kilter. Marybeth's entire body was composed of strange angularities: a thin mouth; one shoulder higher than the other; and, knees akimbo, as though one of Euclid's perfectly symmetrical structures had been rammed by a dozer and hadn't managed to right itself. Maybe my fist could do it.

"Don't you ever touch Lorena again!" I screamed at Marybeth, feeling as self-righteous as a saint for doing the decent thing. Cranking up my right arm for a straight shot, I delivered an uppercut to the llama-like face of my number two stepmother that would have made Mohammed Ali proud of me.

The expression on Mr. Darken's face as Marybeth toppled into him made me aware that it was time for me to make a bargain with a real saint. I prayed to St. Giles, one of the holy helpers, as fast as I could shoot out the "help me now's."

I could see Mother's face brighten with pride as she looked down on her struggling sisterwife and husband just before the platoon led by Enoch and Jerry took me out.

Poised to swoon gracefully and reduce the damage to my body, I flung one arm out to leverage my fall as Enoch hurled himself toward me like a tight end that couldn't decide whether to block or receive. He did both; the socket of my left arm crackled like green wood on a hot fire.

The wood between Enoch's ears might have registered

the fact that my shoulder had taken on an odd configuration. My screech stopped him in his tracks. "You broke my arm! You broke my shoulder! You fucking numbskull!"

I clutched a bent arm against my body. The smallest movement sent waves of pain radiating throughout my shoulder. Such unbearable pain. Perspiration streamed along my cheeks. Or, I might have been weeping. Or laughing.

No one had come to the aid of Marybeth; flat on her back, she was a sight to behold. A pink satin garter belt dating back to the 1950's clutched the thigh-high tops of hose that had seen better days.

Underneath the entire messy affair, stretched past imagining, were Mother's pink lace panties—the same panties I'd borrowed to wear when Josh and I worked on the fence in the canyon.

"Thief!" Mother's voice rang out as loud as though her humerus had just separated from her scapula. The diversion worked. Mr. Darken and Maylene tugged Marybeth to her feet as her face flamed to match Mother's stolen underwear.

Josh's mother pried Jerry's grip off my right arm. "You boys need to leave this girl alone. You've done enough damage to her today. I have to abduct her shoulder. Bonita, you come with us."

A face like a Raphael Madonna peered over Mrs. Barnes's shoulder.

"Bonita Lovelace. Jenny Hatchet. Bonita is visiting from Boise. She's a distant cousin of Marybeth. Staying in the Darken house." All the while Mrs. Barnes talked softly through introductions that didn't interest me in the least, she was edging me away from the crowd, running expert fingers along my arm and gently massaging my shoulder.

I could see Mr. Darken's restraining hand stroking Mother's back as though he might restore equilibrium by wiping off excess humors of melancholy as they did in ancient times. Mother smacked his hand and was at my side in a flash.

"Dislocated. I think I can abduct her shoulder. Kocher's method. It's fallen out of favor, but not too painful if done correctly. She'll be fine, Clara. I'll keep her at my house. Surely Mr. Darken won't object," Mrs. Barnes purred just as my stepfather pushed himself into our little circle, elbowing her rudely.

The low tremolo of Mrs. Barnes' voice echoed like notes of a Gregorian chant that bounce off the walls of a cathedral. It was a sound that defied disagreement.

Her blue eyes glinted with a warning flash at a movement on the edge of the group. Her grip on my arm tightened.

Like a couple of fighting cocks with newly sharpened gaffs, Enoch and Jerry closed ranks the moment they saw Josh Barnes pushing his way through the crowd. He was carrying a wrench the size of my thighbone.

"You got no business here, Josh." Enoch was the first to speak but edged just behind Jerry. "We found the runaway. On the streets of Spokane. We brung her back to Mr. Darken. He has the say-so about the whereabouts of this little lady."

Enoch thumped me gently on my uninjured shoulder, but I sent up a screeching aria as though the pain were unbearable.

The six-inch heel of Mother's Manolo Blahnik planted

itself in Enoch's calf at the same time that Jerry grabbed an Uzi from one of the guards.

Just as he swung the barrel toward Josh, I could feel his mother taking in a great gulp of air as she looked at me with eyes that sent a cryptographer's message—clear as well water.

I flung myself toward Josh, wrapping my only working arm around him and hissed: "Pick me up when I faint."

The pain that shot through my tortured shoulder almost knocked me senseless. The Proustian memory of an odor—the warm, sweaty body of Josh—put me on high alert. It was that scent I remembered from the forest. It was his body that cradled me on the drive to the Reservation.

Snuggled against Josh's chest, I watched Elder Bonner slam the muzzle of Jerry's Uzi down, twist it out of his hands, and elbow both Jerry and Enoch behind him. "We've had enough excitement and foolishness for one day." His stentorian voice split the tension like a bolt of thunder.

"Gomer, take these hysterical women of yours home. Enoch, you and Jerry unload the van. Mrs. Barnes will see to Jenny's injury. Josh, you might as well carry her to your mother's house. She doesn't appear to be mobile."

What I appeared to be was not what I was. With my arm properly anchored to my body, I could still run a 10K. What I couldn't do was detach myself from Josh Barnes. So, I played it to the hilt. *La dame aux Camélias*, beautiful, sexy, desirable, even at death's door.

A dislocated shoulder doesn't lend itself well to operatic fiction. It hurt like hell. I needed to stand up and keep anyone from touching that side of my body.

Through closed eyes, I could feel Josh struggling up porch stairs and hear a door opening and banging shut. I opened my eyes. We were in a room filled with bright hand-thrown pots. Plants hung everywhere, great, blooming plants. Thick sprays of orchids drooped carelessly along window sills.

"Put her on this straight-backed chair. I need her upright for the procedure. Josh, get the pain pills from the bathroom. She'll need them when this is over."

I flinched at the words. I needed them now. I just wanted to be left alone with a large bottle of codeine and Tylenol. Between Jerry's procedure on my neck and Enoch's maneuver with my arm, I was wasted.

Opening my eyes, I glared at Bonita whose face had fixed itself into a beatific, otherworldly expression that had nothing to do with me.

Josh ignored Bonita as he dumped out two pills and shoved them into my hand. "Mother knows what she's doing, Jenny. She trained as a nurse before she and Dad got married. Worked with an orthopedic group in Salt Lake City."

"That was years ago. You overstate my skills, Josh." Mrs. Barnes eased my back against the chair. "I don't think they use Kocher's method on dislocations now, but it works and shouldn't hurt too much, Jenny. Josh, I need you to slowly put traction on her upper arm as I rotate it."

The traction could have gone on forever. The rotation caused wrenching pain for only a moment and then blessed relief as Mrs. Barnes strapped my left arm to my body with a giant swath of dishtowel.

The codeine was kicking in, and I wanted to tell Josh about my mishap in Spokane so he could get word to the Earnshaws. They would be worried about my disappearance.

"You need to lie down, Jenny. You look exhausted." Mrs. Barnes straightened my rhinestone eyeball skull shirt. "What happened to your neck?"

"Jerry's thumbs. I survived them. Abigail didn't." I stood, walked over to the couch, eased down while guarding my shoulder, and fell asleep hearing the soft murmur of Josh's voice telling his mother that I was convinced Abigail Johnson did not drown herself in a cow pond.

CHAPTER 4

Sun streamed through an upstairs window into a strange bedroom. A quilt bright with primary colors humped over a body next to me.

"Jenny, you didn't sleep well last night. You shouted out several times. Something about Abigail. Maylene told me you were a friend of that poor girl. Some of us from our church in Boise came to her funeral. I saw you there, but you seemed preoccupied. Suicide is such a worrisome thing."

Well, that was the understatement of the year. Worrisome, was it? I would set Bonita right. Someone who woke up with her Madonna hair perfectly coiffed, bee-stung pink lips and a name like Lovelace needed to be chopped down a notch.

"Abigail did not commit suicide. She didn't want to marry Jerry. She liked Zeb McAfee. The elders sent him away. A girl's opinion around here isn't worth a tinker's damn." I glowered at Bonita as though she were part of the conspiracy of elders.

"Zeb McAfee? *My* Zeb McAfee?" Bonita's skeptical question sent a flush across her perfect oval face. "He's the reason I . . . my father thought that Cousin Marybeth would be a good influence because I . . ." Bonita's virginal face took on a crafty expression with lips sealed superglue tight.

"I've never seen a girl punch someone like you hit Marybeth. Knocked her right off her feet. Exposed her bloomers to the whole world."

A change of subject wouldn't stop me from finding out why Bonita had been sent from the Boise Compound to this one. I did have a moment of swollen pride for that good right hook and the joy on Mother's face.

"You girls getting acquainted?" Mrs. Barnes pushed the door open and peered inside. "It was a good idea to have Bonita sleep with you last night, Jenny. In case you needed anything. Let's check that shoulder."

My shoulder might have been tie-dyed by a hippie fixated on blue and purple. The white-hot pain of yesterday had simmered into a constant but dull ache.

"You'll need to keep this immobile, Jenny. It's back in place, but your rotator cuff may be torn." Mrs. Barnes prodded my upper arm with one hand while she held a limp ice bag aloft with the other. "No ice. You said you would keep this refilled during the night, Bonita." The accusation in her voice was low-key but pointed.

Time to make nice with Bonita. "She was very helpful, Mrs. Barnes. I slept like a log. I really want to see Mother and Lorena. We had only a minute to speak yesterday before . . ."

"Before you decked Cousin Marybeth who is coming up the walk as we speak." Bonita peered out the bedroom window with a sudden lilt in her voice suggesting that she wanted a ringside seat for my next round.

The explosive sound of fists hitting the front door meant that Marybeth was gloved for action.

Mrs. Barnes smiled sweetly at Bonita who had developed a maddening habit of wringing her hands as though she were the one needing calming.

"I left scrambled eggs and toast on the stove. Would you mind bringing up a tray for Jenny, Bonita? She needs to stay in bed today. Please tell Marybeth I'll be down shortly. She keeps vigil on my house."

The halting reassurance in Mrs. Barnes's voice didn't calm my anxiety. "Vigil" should be a comforting word, accompanied by a prayerful state, the way a parent keeps watch over the bed of a sick child.

Marybeth's vigil took on a new meaning. Like Hitchcock's photographer with a broken leg spying on his murderous neighbor from the rear window, Marybeth would be keeping a very close watch on my broken body. She might also poison my scrambled eggs if she got a chance.

Gently closing the door behind Bonita, Mrs. Barnes sat down on the bed beside me. "We need to talk quickly, Jenny. Marybeth will be up the stairs in a heartbeat. She's the one who insisted that Bonita stay here last night. We don't dare talk in front of either of them."

She flinched as Marybeth's first step resounded on the stairs, and I couldn't resist spouting out:

"Fee-fi-foe-fum, I smell the blood of an Englishman,
Be he live, or be he dead, I'll grind his bones
to make my bread."

A faint cyanotic tinge discolored Mrs. Barnes's cheeks. Her pale, faintly crinkled skin might have been lifted off milk beginning to skim over. Marybeth's vigilance was taking its toll. I wasn't helping by bringing Jack and his beanstalk into the mix.

"Sorry. Just my way of dealing with tension. Drives Mother crazy." I clutched her hand. "Marybeth gives me the creeps. We do need to talk. I'll figure out a way for us to be alone. I'll be careful around Bonita. She might be a spy, but I think she has some secrets of her own."

"Hello, Marybeth!" I shouted in a piercing falsetto as the door burst open and banged shut. "Speak of the devil, and she enters."

"Jenny needs to rest." Mrs. Barnes moved over to block Marybeth from my bedside. "Enoch injured her shoulder badly—though I'm sure it wasn't intentional."

Like a two-step gone off kilter, Mrs. Barnes moved left and right as Marybeth sashayed back and forth, trying to get close enough to gauge my condition.

"If you have other things to do today, we can manage very well, Marybeth," Mrs. Barnes said.

The door creaked open a slit. "I have Jenny's breakfast, Cousin Marybeth. Shall I bring it in?" Bonita's timorous voice queried the person in charge. Marybeth.

I needed to restack the odds. "Warm water. I need to soak my shoulder." I groaned louder than a gut-shot victim in a B movie.

"Jenny needs to soak in warm water for therapy, Marybeth. You and Bonita can wait downstairs, but this will take some time. Getting her into the tub will be tricky. There's really no reason for you to stay."

"There is. Gomer insists. Your groom-to-be, Elder

Grund, insists. *Mi casa su casa*." Marybeth beamed as though she'd just given a Nobel acceptance speech in Spanish—not taken over another woman's house.

"Left out the verb, Marybeth. I'll send you a Spanish dictionary if I find the Get Out of Jail Free card." Needling Marybeth tickled me almost as much as punching her. If I could get that beet-red flush up a notch higher, a classic MI might leave her twitching helplessly on the floor.

No such luck. She latched onto Bonita's arm and steered her out the bedroom door, peppering her with questions. "What do you mean, nothing was said? Nothing? Or nothing you care to repeat? Your pa said you were close-mouthed, secretive. About Zeb. I heard all about that. No reason to hold your tongue around me. Licking a bar of Lifebuoy soap will cure that habit."

"Marybeth missed her calling by being born five hundred years too late," I whispered to Mrs. Barnes who looked at me with a blank expression. "The Inquisition. Like the Grand Inquisitor Torquemada, she's got the answer before she asks the question."

THE OLD-FASHIONED claw-footed tub provided an upright back that was perfect for maneuvering down into it with one arm. Over the noise of running water, Mrs. Barnes and I could talk.

"Josh was planning to leave a message for Heath last night in their secret location—that old tree house just beyond the blackberry thicket. It's risky for Josh to get out of the SYM quarters." Mrs. Barnes lowered her voice, fearful that Marybeth might have crept back to listen outside of the door. "They watch every move he makes. That was quick thinking yesterday, Jenny. Pretending to faint so that Josh could catch you. I was afraid of what Jerry might do with that gun. It was very clever of you."

I nodded, sinking as far down as possible in the warm water, watching my elbow drift up without the excruciating pain of normal movement. Not daring to look Josh's mother in the eye, I feared that she might see duplicity brewing. I could have blocked Jerry's gun by standing. I chose to fall into Josh's arms.

Heath had told me that Josh was confined in SYM— Single Young Men. It was a makeshift dormitory for the older boys whose fathers weren't on the ruling Council and didn't have the resources to set up their sons with a wife and a homestead.

Sometimes other Compounds accepted promising young men just to bring in new blood. Maylene once let it slip that the CPRC kept a Consanguinity Table. I envisioned it as something like the tablets of Moses, a list of "thou shalt nots" to keep cousins from nuzzling cousins and breeding babies for freak shows.

I reached up a toe and turned on the hot water tap. Lovely. I could stay here forever. No chance of drowning with Mrs. Barnes watching me like a mother duck.

Those pale blue, perpetually guarded eyes were luminous this morning. A rope of blond hair streaked with silver formed a figure eight at the back of her neck. As a young woman, she must have been stunningly beautiful. Her loose-fitting, drab clothes and retiring manner were disguises.

I thought about how the Count of Monte Cristo had sewn himself into a shroud to escape prison and returned in multiple disguises to wreak vengeance on his persecutors.

Vengeance occupied me night and day—when I wasn't letting Enoch break my bones. The woman carefully kneading my shoulder might know a great deal about disguises even though an eye for an eye didn't seem to be part of her theology.

She had helped Mother bake me an ugly pottery pendant to hide the two-caret diamond Mr. Darken had put on her finger—after it had been on Maylene's and then Marybeth's. The nest egg from that ring sat safely in a bank in Spokane under Aunt Izzy's name.

Mrs. Barnes had disguised forty feet of paracord as a macramé plant holder so that I could rappel down three floors of the Winner's house. This woman in her drab homespun dresses knew the art of disguise. I was skilled in the craft of revenge. I flexed the fist at the end of my good arm. Contact with Marybeth's whiskery chin had felt delicious.

Smokescreens and paybacks. Mrs. Barnes and I might make a good team. I flashed her a helpless smile. "My left arm is useless. If you can help me get out of the tub, I'll start making a list of dirty tricks to get us out of the hoosegow."

Her spontaneous, ear-to-ear grin reminded me so much of Josh that I said to myself: *her son can come along for the ride.*

CHAPTER 5

"Helen! Griselda's here! Time for Elder Grund's therapy. I'll stay with Jenny!" Marybeth's foghorn voice could eliminate the need for lighthouses.

"No she won't; I'm going with you," I hissed to Helen, hearing her given name for the first time. Of course, she'd be named after the most beautiful woman in history.

Mother's parents named her for the famous silent screen star, the "It" girl, Clara Bow. Odd how real life turns on itself. At a young age, Clara Bow had to take care of her mother; my mother looked like a movie star, but I needed to take care of her.

"Griselda's here! She's waiting for you, Helen, and getting very impatient!"

"Griselda, as in Chaucer's tales?" I asked Mrs. Barnes.

"Misnamed, as you noticed," she responded wryly. "She's always impatient."

Wrapped in a big towel, I peered over the stair rail to see why someone would name that fidgety, sour-faced woman below after the patient Griselda.

Chaucer's Griselda bore her husband's bullying past all imagining. He spirited away both her children at birth and showed her a phony annulment of their marriage when he brought her daughter back years later as his intended new wife.

I decided to try a bit of bullying myself. "I'm just finishing my therapy at the moment, Marybeth. Surely it's not too much to ask Mrs. Grund to wait for a few minutes. You could whip up one of your nice puddings for her."

Marybeth's puddings could fell an entire army with dysentery, but Mr. Darken galloped through them with obvious pleasure. Maybe Griselda Grund had the same ironclad constitution.

Mrs. Barnes latched onto my good arm, pulling me back from the rail. "Careful, Jenny. No one trifles with the Grunds. They're connected to the founding family through marriage with special status and considerable power."

She leaned over the rail. "We'll be down right away, Griselda. I need to get the blood pressure cuff. Jenny can walk with us and work on her therapy."

She turned a pleading face toward me. "Just try to be like the long-suffering Griselda, Jenny. At the Grund house, don't speak unless someone speaks to you. The first wife Magdalene probably won't show herself. If she does, try not to be alarmed."

Like an engine with the gears disconnected, the face of Mrs. Barnes had settled back into passivity. I remembered her pained expression when Marybeth said she was keeping vigil at the house per Elder Grund's orders.

That old man gave too many orders. Before I made my escape from the Compound, Elder Grund had uncovered the stash of batteries that I'd convinced Mr. Darken to buy—thereby spoiling my plot to fry saints on the electric fence. He was in the group of elders who had drugged and carted me up to the Winner attic.

When he confronted me about my plans for an amped electric fence with his persimmon-puckered mouth, Elder Grund appeared to be about a hundred years old.

Even with Mrs. Barnes's therapy, the stent for his ancient ticker hadn't given him a new lease on life. Heath had told me that the elders were going to force Mrs. Barnes into marriage with Elder Grund so that she could become his caretaker—all her land and the house would become his.

That would leave Josh penniless and at the mercy of other compounds looking for good breeding stock. Through the pain of a dislocated shoulder yesterday, I had noticed Bonita Lovelace sidling up alongside of Josh when he was carrying me. If Zeb McAfee had been put off limits, she might have her eye on a new prize.

Bonita would have no competition from me. I looked at the drab gray dress on my bed. My sparkly skull top and thigh-high skirt were nowhere to be seen.

"Learn to blend in, Jenny. And listen. Like a Cold War British spy in one of Le Carré's novels." For a moment, Mrs. Barnes sounded like Aunt Izzy, trying to make a fictional world real.

Nuclear espionage seemed a bit more sporting than stumbling around with a damaged shoulder looking for a hole in the fence.

Or a tunnel under it. I just remembered Heath telling me about rumors of a tunnel that the early settlers had discovered to protect themselves from Indian raids. Supposedly, the tunnel became a secret place for stores—known only to the senior elder and his oldest son. World War I claimed the oldest son, and the news of his death caused the elder's fatal stroke. The location of the tunnel—if it ever existed—was lost forever.

AS I TRAILED Mrs. Barnes and Griselda Grund across the field toward a bluff, I thought hopefully about strokes—Elder Grund's in particular. Considering his lack of skills as the Compound electrician, he might get a volt that would rupture an artery—or melt his stent.

I watched Josh's mother picking her way gracefully along a path that led up a steep incline. She snapped off a stem with small white flowers: "Peppergrass. When the pods fill out, the seeds make an interesting pepper substitute."

Substitute. That's what these women settled for. Something that replaced a real life. Here was Josh's lovely mother on her way to help Elder Grund who was plotting a marriage to seize her property and disinherit her son.

The nightmare of imprisonment that these women were born into didn't end in a trumped up celestial marriage. That was just another kind of villainy, suggesting that the earthly union was so glorious it needed to go on into eternity.

I thought about being handed off to Jerry or to Enoch. The Jenny Hatchet I knew would simply cease to exist. I'd be an "other," not even an appendage that comes with being happily married. I'd be part of the herd, one of the mares. No. They were free to run. I'd be like one of those fenced-in ewes that bump constantly against the enclosure, always on the verge of madness.

Just as we reached the top of the hill, I stopped in disbelief. Like a facsimile of the House of Usher, a two-story phantasmagorical structure loomed before us. Turrets sprouted out of the roof like a ring of fairy mushrooms.

A miasmic morning fog hung over the house, turning its nooks and crannies into shifting shadows.

Then, one of the shadows moved away from a side door and waved. Vigorously, as though it were trying to flag us down before we moved a step closer to the house.

Billows of lime green satin tumbled forward, head over heels, and landed in a heap just at the edge of the porch. A head covered with what appeared to be steel wool popped up out of the folds.

"I saw you before you saw me. Marching up the hill like Dumas' three musketeers. Two musketeers. Griselda doesn't count. She never has." The cackle coming out of a mouth filled with blue gums and an odd assortment of ragged teeth grated like fingernails on a blackboard.

Mrs. Barnes extended her hand and lifted the woman to her feet. "Hello, Magdalene. Jenny, this is Magdalene Grund. Magdalene, I've not seen you in ages."

"Rock of Ages, cleft for me. Cleft my foot. Let me hide myself in thee." She cackled again. "Let me hide myself from him." She thrust a thumb at the house.

"Old bugger's up to no good. If you value your pudendum—or this pretty girl's here—you'll scoot back down the hill."

My mouth dropped ajar farther than that old crone's. I couldn't believe my ears. Bugger. Pudendum. Words like that coming from the senior sisterwife of an important elder?

"You hush your nasty mouth this minute, Magdalene. This girl is new to the Compound. You're making a bad impression on her." Griselda swatted at Magdalene who swerved like an expert avoider.

"She's not new. Her name is Jenny Hatchet. She runs faster than a streak of lightning. Caused a small riot in the prison." If her face could be twisted into a semblance of sympathy, I knew that was the look she sent me.

Darting behind Mrs. Barnes, Magdalene moved beside me and grabbed my arm. My good arm. Her grasp was surprisingly tender. Her scratchy voice wasn't. "Your mother got hoodwinked by Gomer Darken. Your little sister has been farmed out to the Johnsons. They won't harm her."

"Someone is going to harm you if you don't get back into the house, Magdalene. I'm calling for the help if you don't go inside now!" Griselda's arms waved like spastic windmills at two boys chopping brush along one side of the house.

With a surprising show of strength for an old woman—and one hampered by a costume that Marie Antoinette might have worn before she was caged—Magdalene pulled me with her to the edge of the porch.

"Act scared," she hissed softly. "Act scared when I show you something. Fear can be used to your advantage. That way no one suspects we're best friends. Tomorrow night. Bottom of the hill. I'll bring you something. It's a way out."

With that, she shoved me away, climbed up on the porch and yanked off an oddly shaped leather boot. I tried not to gasp at the sight. Her big toe was fused to the second toe with a deep, inch-wide space between the next three fused toes.

"Cleft of the devil. Rock of ages. Cleft for me. Daughter of the devil." Her squawks trailed behind her as two burly boys lifted her up and carried her through the front door.

Griselda followed with a stream of "just you wait until our husband hears . . ." The door slammed as we stood in stunned silence.

CHAPTER 6

As we stared at the closed door, Mrs. Barnes touched my hand. "I'm sorry you had to see her like that, Jenny. Elder Grund has told everyone that she is schizophrenic. He once took her to a psychiatrist in Spokane for drugs. They don't seem to work—or she isn't taking them. Or she's acting out for a reason. Magdalene is not always what she seems."

I didn't respond. I was too busy thinking about Magdalene's whispered words to me. In the midst of her crazy behavior, she had pulled me aside so that no one else could hear her. She might be mentally ill, but there was a kind of canny awareness in her eyes that unsettled me more than her madness.

"Wait out here, Jenny. You can sit on the porch swing and enjoy the beautiful vista. This was the first big house built here in the late 1870s by Magdalene's great-grandfather Daniel Marchman. He was with a splinter group that parted company with Brigham Young before the wagon train reached the Great Salt Lake Valley." Mrs. Barnes sighed.

"The official story is that the quarrel had something to

do with a new surveyor named Taylor who had shown up with a wagon full of equipment, sextants, telescopes and the like. Daniel Marchman had packed his own surveying tools all the way from Illinois—old brass and wooden things. Magdalene still has them. I think the split had to do with theology. By 1844, Prophet Brigham was accumulating so many wives I doubt he could sort them out."

The vision of so many sisterwives quarreling like crows over a slice of the mutton-whiskered Brigham Young prompted me to ask a dozen questions. I turned toward Mrs. Barnes, but she had disappeared quietly into Elder Grund's asylum.

I settled for the spectacular view from the highest house in the Compound. From the cusp of the mountains to the flatlands as far as I could see, every plot of tilled land was a perfect rectangle. From the vantage point of Magdalene's porch, a remarkable pattern spread out below me.

Every lot might contain a different style of house and a different number of outbuildings, but each parcel was cordoned off from its neighbor by a fence or hedge. Perfect isosceles triangles nestled side by side, one triangle offering a big backyard and the neighboring one a big front yard.

Like common fields in England, pastures spread out beyond the clusters of houses.

I wanted to know more about this long-dead surveyor, this great-grandfather of Magdalene. He had geometry on the brain. In places where the terrain was so rugged that a straight or symmetrically curved line seemed impossible, triangles, circles, and rectangles nested in perfect union.

The gentle back and forth motion of the porch swing

lulled me into a drowsy state in which the scent of fir trees made me think of past Christmases—happy times before Scrooge's ghost showed me a future behind an electric fence.

Just as his chains rattled, the swing stopped abruptly. "Helen asked me to bring you a drink so you don't get dehydrated. Altitude can be a problem for newcomers." Griselda shoved a sweating glass of something filled with lemon slices toward me.

I gratefully gulped what tasted like nectar fit for the gods. Lemonade with a kind of sweetness that wasn't quite like sugar. "Wonderful! I've never tasted such lemonade."

"My special honey. I do the beekeeping. No one else is allowed to touch the hives," she said with a note of pride. The crinkles between her eyes smoothed out as she pointed toward rows of stacked boxes in a small field to the south of the porch. A steep bluff of rock that resembled stony honeycomb sheltered the beehives from harsh winds.

"Hives have been here since Magdalene's great-grandpa laid claim to this place. Old Indian graveyard was by those funny rocks. No signs of anything like nice tombstones. They just let the birds pick at the bodies back then, way before any of us come along. Savage practice. I didn't think the bees would thrive so near to that evil place."

From the edge of the porch, Griselda waved a limp hand toward the hives like the grieving Victoria acknowledging her subjects from afar. "Years ago, I moved them closer, hive by hive, very slowly so as not to disturb them too much. I didn't lose a single colony," she said, jutting out her jaw with pride.

Find the hobby, and you'll find the hook. I shot my most

disarming smile toward Griselda. "Do you have time to tell me about beekeeping, Mrs. Grund? I find bees fascinating insects." Actually, having been stung on the ankle when running through a patch of clover, I give bees a wide berth.

"Griselda. You can call me Griselda. My maiden name was Simmons. I always liked my maiden name." Shifting her hips from side to side as though the swing might flex to accommodate her sizeable rear end, she settled down beside me.

"The queen bee rules—commanding anywhere from thirty to fifty thousand female worker bees and the drones." She pointed toward a small swarm of bees hovering over spears of lavender alongside the front porch. "When a primed queen takes flight, she may mate with dozens of drones, then lay over three thousand eggs a day."

A shadow moved across Griselda's face. All that lust and fertility seemed to depress her into silence. I changed the subject to keep her talking.

"Don't they try to sting when you take the honeycombs? I'd be frightened to touch one of their hives." *Weakness of body and mind needed to be my ploy now. Let Griselda sit in the catbird's seat.*

She took the bait. "Confidence. It takes confidence. Bees sense fear. I use fir needles in my smoker. It's a scent they know, so they settle right down. Never been stung once. Not once."

I was just about to launch into the queen bee topic again—though I already knew from my biology class that the queen bee releases pheromones to put the other female bees' ovaries on hold—when Griselda planted both feet and pushed back the swing, heaving herself up with some effort.

"I need to check on how Mrs. Barnes is doing with Cyrus. It's too quiet in there," she added.

Hopping to my feet, I hoped that I could get inside that mausoleum. If the inside of the house was anything like the outside, it would make a dandy setting for a horror movie. "What kind of therapy does Mrs. Barnes provide?" That seemed like an innocent question.

"Nothing that I can't do!" she barked at me. "He walks on the treadmill, and she takes his blood pressure. She gives him a list of foods cooked without lard. He won't eat them, so I put the lard back. Can't make a biscuit or piecrust without lard. Not flaky," she sniffed indignantly.

I gazed at her sympathetically. Whether she knew it or not, Griselda was on my side. I could envision little clusters of plaque chasing up Elder Grund's arteries with each bite of flaky crust.

At the front door, Griselda firmly pushed me back. "Best to stay outside, Jenny. Magdalene is in a bad way this morning. She was born crippled. Hobbles around like a cart with a missing wheel," she added smugly.

"As a girl she mostly got around on horses. Her pa bought her anything she ever wanted. Fancy clothes from the city. That big black piano all the way from San Francisco. Anything that selfish girl desired." Griselda was now talking to me through the screen door, as though the venom in her voice should be filtered.

"A looker back then. Wouldn't know that to see her now. Turned Cyrus into a blithering idiot. He couldn't see other girls for her." Griselda plucked at the tension bar across the screen as though thumbing a harp to sweeten her spite.

"We all thought she might have had polio in that leg—and her folks were too embarrassed to say. She was sickly as a small child. Never ever took off her boots."

Griselda pressed her lips to the screen. "Her pa put it in the marriage agreement with Cyrus: Boot stays on when everything else comes off unless she says different."

I backed away from the screen as though the rancor coming out of her mouth might be contagious.

"The day after her pa's funeral, Cyrus tied her down so he could see what was inside that boot. That's when he came looking for me. I was a plain girl but normal. Two years of sleeping with the devil cured him of lust."

The note of disappointment I heard in her voice suggested that Cyrus Grund never contracted the disease of lust again. The door slammed in my face.

Then opened. "Sorry, Jenny. It took longer than I expected. Elder Grund isn't very compliant with his cardiac rehab program." Mrs. Barnes hurried across the porch and down the stairs without a single glance back.

I hurried forward, linking my arm through hers. "I heard. He has an addiction to pig fat. Griselda's piecrusts and biscuits, but he doesn't get off on a malformed foot of the devil."

Mrs. Barnes skidded to a stop. "I can't believe you said that, Jenny."

"I didn't. Griselda did. Well, not in those words, but she told me Magdalene's father married her off with the caveat that Cyrus Grund would never remove her boot. He died, and Cyrus did."

"Syndactyly, Jenny. Fused toes. She was born that way. Double first cousins on both sides. Surgery would take care of it today, but back then her parents feared to let anyone see her foot. Some of our people look for signs of the devil—especially in a newborn. Old superstitions die hard."

Mrs. Barnes steered me ahead of her down the incline as she talked. "I've seen photographs of Magdalene as a young girl. She was a beauty. Quite a horsewoman in her heyday. They say she never came across a fence she couldn't jump or a canyon too steep to ride down. Neither she nor Griselda bore a child."

Josh's mother sent me a plaintive glance. I suspected that she was thinking of Josh. I needed to change the subject before I got gloomy with her.

"According to Griselda, Cyrus came looking for a new wife after he unshod Magdalene. On the titillation scale, Griselda probably never tickled anyone's fancy. Makes good biscuits though." I was hoping to cheer up Josh's mother with a witticism. Sometimes I noticed a wry sense of humor lurking, afraid to surface.

She stalked ahead of me, bent over, as though the trek back down the mountain was exhausting her. Apparently, my sense of levity regarding the saints struck a sour note. I needed to restore myself to her good graces.

"I make flippant remarks, because I don't know how to be normal in this place, Mrs. Barnes. You're normal. Josh is normal. Maylene might be just this side of normal if she didn't try to make everything rhyme. But this place is a zoo. My mother may be hooked on Valium. My little sister is being indoctrinated by people I barely know." I was running out of words. I did have lots of suppressed tears, so I let them flow.

Mrs. Barnes pulled me down onto a fallen Douglas fir and wiped my cheeks with the corner of her apron. "I wasn't trying to ignore you, Jenny. I was deep in my own worries. This place *has* become a zoo."

She looked off into the distance before speaking. "When my parents and my husband's parents were growing up here, this was a small religious community. Neighbors cared for one another. Except for a few of the earliest settlers' families, most of the marriages were monogamous."

She paused and scowled. "Things changed. The Bonners, the Winners, and, later, the Darkens moved in from other communities and bought out the small farmers. Formed a different corporation. Caused issues involving joint ventures that had been in place for decades with the Reservation. Now, all these guns and a kind of persecution complex about the outside world . . ." she stopped abruptly.

Her hands were trembling. I clutched both of them with my good hand. "Over a year ago, Josh's father and I made a decision to leave. First, he had to get things sorted. Things that shouldn't have been . . ." her words trailed off as she stared down the long, winding path before us. "I feel as though the bottom has dropped out of the life I knew. Sam dying like that . . ." Mrs. Barnes's eyelids dropped for an instant as though she had to block the image of her husband being gored by a bull.

When she opened those sky blue eyes, so like Josh's, I imagined I could see flashes of lightning behind them. "They keep my son away from me. Someone is always spying. Now, today, Cyrus Grund—a man I've known all my life—acted as bizarre as Magdalene. He actually put his hand on my thigh. Purposefully."

The timbre of her voice registered more shock over Cyrus's roving hand than the recollection of her husband impaled on a bull's horns. *The days of Cyrus's goring were over, but it didn't seem timely to mention it now.*

As I pulled Mrs. Barnes to her feet, she placed her hands on both sides of my face. "My paranoia escalated so much that when Gomer Darken brought your mother, you and Lorena here, I feared that you were brought to spy on us. The first time I saw you running around the Compound, I warned Josh."

She planted a resounding kiss on my cheek. "Stupid of me. I know that Gomer Darken victimized your mother. Lorena is a little charmer. And you, Jenny. You've given me hope."

Between the pain in my shoulder, the bizarre introduction to Magdalene, and the burden of hope that Mrs. Barnes had just unloaded on me, I needed to fall into a bed and sleep until sanity woke me.

Sanity would make us as we used to be–Mother, giddy as a teenager with a new pair of shoes, Lorena pouting if we weren't giving her our undivided attention, and my father gone into eternity where he might come across Euclid and discuss postulates.

CHAPTER 7

A pouty Madonna stepped right out of Bellini's painting and through my bedroom door, looking very determined, as though she had seen the future and intended to change history.

"Jenny, you rat! You two-faced sneak!"

I pushed myself up against the headboard, wrapped my good arm protectively across my bad shoulder, and bent my knees judo fashion in case Bonita Lovelace came any closer. "Are you out of your mind? What in the world did I do to you?"

"Told Marybeth all kinds of things about me. About Zeb McAfee. About how he broke the token of troth between that mush-wouldn't-melt-in-her-mouth Abigail Johnson and Jerry Winner. About how I've got the hots for Josh Barnes. If my pa gets wind of anything from Marybeth, I'm dead." Bonita did appear a bit lifeless after her outburst.

"Let's just get something straight, you dimwit. I don't gossip." Self-righteousness always sets the stage to put someone in a defensive posture. Actually, I found gossip a fruitful pastime but needed to set Bonita straight by sidestepping the issue.

"And, if I did spill the beans, I wouldn't talk to that child-abuser Marybeth." I aimed a middle finger at the sound of pots banging around in the kitchen downstairs.

"She's down there as we speak telling Helen Barnes that things will be settled between her and Elder Grund in a week, as soon as she finds the deed to her property and signs it over." Bonita now seemed reassured enough to rat out Marybeth.

"Finds the deed?" I was catching a whiff of intrigue that Bonita was missing.

"Oh. Some old papers that her husband put somewhere. I heard Mr. Darken talking to Marybeth and Maylene about the fact that after statehood, the CPRC quit filing changes in land ownership officially because it was an internal matter. Seems that the original filed deed showed both sets of the Barnes's parents owning land that the Bonners and Winners now farm." Bonita grinned slyly. "I can listen at keyholes too, Jenny."

I rolled carefully out of bed and shot Bonita a companionable smile. She might be a nitwit, but she was good at eavesdropping.

Somehow, I had to get this information to Josh. I doubted that a legal issue would stop the saints from their stratagem to swindle Mrs. Barnes out of her property, but it might give Josh an ace up his sleeve.

Sparkling with unspoken devices, I sauntered downstairs and beamed across the kitchen at Marybeth who had resumed her interrogation of Mrs. Barnes. I glanced at her wrists and ankles checking for shackles. "No *strappado* today, huh, Marybeth? Torture by soup?"

"Stra-what, you silly girl? Speak the king's English." Marybeth turned toward the stove and gave a stir to something vile boiling on it.

"Mrs. Barnes and I are having a civilized conversation. You and Bonita go check the coop for eggs. Make yourselves useful." Marybeth could snap out orders faster than a Marine drill instructor.

"I don't think that Jenny is quite fit for ..." Mrs. Barnes eyed me gripping my bad side.

"This sling you made for me last night helps stabilize my shoulder very well, Mrs. Barnes. I just need the straps tightened. If you could show Bonita, then she could do it."

I edged Marybeth aside, turning so that she couldn't see my face and winked at Mrs. Barnes. I had to get out of the house, away from Marybeth's spying eyes and figure out a way to contact Josh.

By including Bonita in my plans, I could keep an eye on her and possibly make her a double agent. I might need her help getting out of the house tonight to meet Magdalene Grund at the bottom of the hill to find out what she wanted to give me.

Grasping Bonita's hand as though we had just become great comrades, I avoided her grateful cow eyes. She seemed like a needy kind of girl—not one I'd toady to if I had any choice.

I had no intention of letting Bonita in on my scheme to meet Magdalene later tonight, but I might conspire with Josh to lead her astray. If I could put her in a compromising position, the Madonna might be a perfect mole.

"My shoulder is feeling so much better, Mrs. Barnes;

I can help you work on a better filing system today. We talked about me helping you sort out things in your office, finishing the project that Josh started." There. I'd dropped two broad hints: documents and Josh.

Like a counter espionage agent, Mrs. Barnes picked up the clues and breezed ahead. "That's wonderful, Jenny. My office is a mess. Recipes and devotional tracts that I've been collecting for years. Clutter everywhere."

Clever woman. Recipes and devotional tracts were probably Marybeth's idea of a good read. Nothing unusual to pique her interest.

"Until you bring me them eggs, you girls are not to leave the premises. I'm making egg salad. It's washday. We always have egg salad sandwiches on washday. This time, put bluing in the sheets, Helen. They've gotten downright yellow."

Mrs. Barnes bore the criticism like a trooper and responded with a bright smile. "Your housekeeping skills become you, Marybeth. My house has never been so clean since you took over custodial duties."

The double-edged comment zipped right past Marybeth who probably considered being a warden as equal in status to her Marine DI persona.

"I'm out of Mrs. Stewart's Bluing. Maybe Bonita and Jenny could pop over to Mrs. Johnson's house to get a bottle after they gather the eggs?" Mrs. Barnes's question was tentative, as though she knew the answer.

"I only let Jenny go with you to the Grund house yesterday because Griselda was along. These girls are *not* supposed to get out of my *jurisdiction*."

Big word for Marybeth. Took in both legal and territorial dimensions of our lives. "I'm crippled, Marybeth, thanks to you and Enoch. How do you think I could get very far in this condition?" I moved my stiff shoulder and groaned for effect as she ignored me.

Then, I tried another tactic. "You are causing me to break one of the Ten Commandments, Marybeth."

She whirled away from stirring the pot on the stove and glared at me. "I never in my life did such a thing."

"Honor thy mother. Right there in the Bible. I haven't seen her since the day before yesterday. I consider that extreme dishonor when I'm less than a mile away from her." I puffed up like a defensive frog.

"She's right, Marybeth. It's not Christian to keep family members apart. When Jenny and Bonita pick up the bluing at the Johnson house, Jenny can see Lorena and then drop by your house to visit a bit with Clara. Maylene will be there. What's the harm?"

Without waiting for a response, Mrs. Barnes opened the back door. "Egg basket is on the back stoop. Don't get the eggs with an "x" on them. Just leave the basket on the back porch. I'll boil and shell them for Marybeth. No one makes egg salad like she does."

Considering Marybeth's culinary skills, I knew that last comment to be a fine backhanded whack. I also knew that if Bonita and I cut across the pasture behind the Johnson's house, we might come across Josh working horses. I had watched him from my prison in the Winner attic. My only respite from the *Book of Mormon*.

I shoved Bonita out the door and snatched up the basket.

"You get the eggs; I'll hold the basket." By now, Bonita had grown accustomed to having orders barked at her.

She moved listlessly toward the hencoops and shoved those beady-eyed, hook-billed chickens aside as though she were oblivious to being mauled by a cross-tempered hen. I had found a use for this farm girl after all.

MRS. JOHNSON CLASPED me to her bosom like a long-lost daughter. "Jenny, I worried about you constantly after you left. The forest is a dangerous place. I wouldn't want my child . . ."

She stopped abruptly and stared into space. Both of us knew that is exactly where her daughter was. Six feet under the shade of a giant Douglas fir on the edge of a boreal forest.

Stumbling around in the darkness the night I made my escape, I had come upon the graveyard just outside the Compound. On that cold night, the mound of fresh dirt that marked my friend Abigail's grave comforted me in an odd way.

I needed to repay the favor. "I told Abigail I missed her. It consoled me to be with her for a while that night I ran away."

Mrs. Johnson nodded as though I'd said nothing out of the ordinary. To her, talking to the dead wasn't in the least bizarre. I had held one-way conversations with my father often during the past year. The dead simply die into us if we allow them. They don't have to disappear. Mrs. Johnson knew that as well as I did.

"Jenny! Jenny! You've come to get me! I knew you would!" Two arms and two legs wound themselves around me, heedless of the fact that a broken shoulder protested the affection.

"Lorena, Jenny can't pick you up. She has a hurt shoulder." Mrs. Johnson gently peeled Lorena away.

"Band-Aids. Barbie Band-Aids. That will fix her up in a flash. Oh. Forgot. She kicked that Barbie suitcase Mr. Darken gave her clear across the room. Better try plain ones."

Lorena was tugging on my arm all the time she was chattering away. "You can watch me pack." She nodded at Bonita. "She can come too. I don't know your name. You'd look nice in Jenny's skull shirt." She frowned at Bonita's 1950s skirt and blouse, poised to give her a fashion appraisal.

Mrs. Johnson steered her toward the kitchen. "Lorena, we can fix cocoa for your sister and Bonita if you'll set out the cups and saucers the way I taught you, like a grown-up girl."

Lorena shook off her hand, turned toward me with a grin, and skipped ahead of Mrs. Johnson singing: "Oh, darling, don't you ever grow up, don't you ever grow up . . ." Taylor Swift hadn't deserted Lorena even though Mother and I had.

"It's time, Jenny. Cousin Marybeth will be banging on the door if we don't finish our errand. She said we had one hour to get the bluing to her—that would allow plenty of time for you to see your sister and mother. Marybeth is a fiend about watching clocks." Bonita nudged me for the second time in so many minutes.

"Fan of Harrison or Sully, is she?" Bonita gave me a blanker look than the one that usually adorned her face. "Clockmakers. In the 1700s, Harrison made fine longcase clocks; Sully invented the gridiron pendulum. Marvelous the way that it . . ."

Bonita interrupted. "Who cares about old clocks? I'll get in trouble if we're not back in an hour, Jenny."

I cared about old clocks. Repairing clocks and selling them to antique stores as "mint vintage," whatever that was supposed to mean, was a hobby my father and I shared. All those lovely gears and springs working in unison. Nothing but the cogs of unease worked behind Bonita's muddy brown eyes.

Leaving Lorena behind would have brought tears to my eyes if I hadn't watched Mrs. Johnson stroking her flaxen hair, wrapping curls around her finger, patting her shoulder lovingly, and never saying a word about sharing airwaves with Taylor Swift.

When we reached the Darken house, seeing Mother reminded me of Tennyson's lady of Shalott watching life through a mirror: "til her blood was frozen slowly, and her eyes were darken'd wholly."

Bonita burst through the door that Maylene held open so that Mother didn't see me at first. She sat sunken into a brown floral chair in the living room with a skein of yarn, eyeing two wooden knitting needles as though she might be considering impaling herself on them.

The minute she spotted me, color flushed her cheeks like late summer roses. "Jenny. Jenny. Jenny." The sound of her voice was as comforting as a warm bath on my tortured shoulder.

"Gomer agreed to bring me to Mrs. Barnes's house this evening for a visit with you, just to check on your shoulder. And here you are! We can have two visits today."

The treat of a second visit supervised by Gomer Darken gave me acid reflux for two reasons: he generated murderous impulses by being in the same room; and, I had a prior engagement tonight with the madwoman on the hill.

I needed to talk to Mother in a language that neither Maylene nor Bonita would understand. Maylene had tactfully moved back into the kitchen, but Bonita, all ears, had plopped down in a chair next to us.

"We can't stay long, Mother. Marybeth's inner alarm is set for one hour from the time we left Mrs. Barnes's house. My shoulder is much better, and Lorena is fine. We stopped by to see her."

Mother nibbled at her bottom lip as though she were restraining it from screaming for help, but her eyes didn't have that Valium fog I was fearful of seeing.

"Tonight won't work very well, Mother. Mrs. Barnes is firing up her kiln. She promised to show me a new line of pottery—she's putting white daisies on it."

Mother's eyes widened just for a moment, then closed briefly. She was up to speed. When she had baked Mr. Darken's diamond ring into an ugly pottery pendant for me, she painted a droopy daisy on it. The proceeds from that ring were safe at Aunt Izzy's bank—our little nest egg if we ever got our own henhouse again.

"We really need to head back, Jenny. Marybeth will be out of sorts if we are late." Bonita was standing by the door, wringing her hands in that Pontius Pilate mode again.

"When is Marybeth *never* out of sorts?" I responded to no one in particular but saw Maylene peeking through the kitchen door with a sly grin on her face. I nestled against Mother. She seemed so frail, so weathered by imprisonment.

As she self-consciously tucked her feet back under the chair, I was almost knocked sideways by the gleam of the new black snakeskin pumps on her feet. Monolo Blahnik had found Northern Idaho.

Too stunned to give her credit for tasteful footwear she must have finagled out of Mr. Darken, I gave her some cryptic news that wouldn't mean anything to anyone else.

"Uncle Hal says I look just like my Grandmother Hatchet, but I think he's still too miffed about things to feel kinship."

Mother's quick intake of breath had peaked Bonita's interest. Like a decent espionage agent, Bonita picked up on body language quickly. I had no intention of airing family laundry in front of her, but I was spiteful enough to want to give Mother a dressing down for keeping family history from me. She had told me I had an uncle only as my father was being dropped into a grave in Portland.

"My friends from the Reservation and I paid Uncle Hal a short visit. Scared the bejesus out of me when I saw him walking down the street. You neglected to mention the spitting image detail, Mother." I smiled down at her as she began shredding the yarn into tiny streamers of wool.

"No matter. Just thought you'd like an update on your brother-in-law. I doubt that he'll be paying a visit." I said that for Maylene's benefit. She had tucked herself back into the doorframe, but I could see her reflection in the window and knew she was sopping up information like a sponge. I doubted that she'd share it with Mr. Darken. Of his wives, Marybeth was the town crier.

I gave Mother a one-armed hug and whispered. "Don't worry. I have a plan." I didn't but I needed to restore the light in her eyes that I'd just managed to extinguish by mentioning Uncle Hal. Guilt, I suppose. She'd dumped my father's identical twin brother without so much as a single verse of fare-thee-well.

CHAPTER 8

Bonita and I had just circled the backside of the community barn when the Greek god of light and sun took off his shirt in front of us. Bonita was enough of a hayseed to gasp and screech "Hi, Josh," as she crossed her arms like a penitent getting ready to receive communion.

With one arm out of commission, I flung my right hand in the air, waving it limply, when I really wanted to swat Bonita. Stealth was what we needed to be about—not grade school giggling.

The horse on the end of a lunge line kept circling the corral with Josh anchored in the middle. I noted his sharp, quick glances around to be sure that no one was in sight.

"Bonita, could you go stand by the corner of the barn and keep a lookout for anyone coming this way?"

Bonita's pouty expression could rival Lorena's at the candy counter when Mother said no. I would offer her a candy-coated fib. "Get over there quickly, Bonita! You don't want anyone to see you talking to Josh. They might get the right idea."

That sailed over her head, but she clung to my side like a limpet. "He can't take his eyes off you, but he's afraid to be seen talking to you, Bonita. Maybe I can help."

Judas Iscariot couldn't have been slicker—except I couldn't bring myself to plant a kiss on her cheek.

As I opened the corral gate, Josh reined in the horse and whipped it around so that we were partially shielded from prying eyes.

He tentatively touched my sling. "Enoch will suffer. I promise you that, Jenny."

His smile seemed open, almost guileless, but a second of hesitation made me wonder if he didn't want that kind of intimacy. Didn't trust those kinds of feelings or did he simply not trust me?

"It doesn't matter, Josh. By the way, I didn't thank you for helping me escape. I was stupid to get caught again." I smiled ruefully up at him, remembering how he had taken me to safety on the Reservation. Ill and barely conscious, I had barfed all over myself and was foul at the nether end from drinking noxious water in the forest. I hoped he had a faulty memory.

"We need to talk quickly. Spies are everywhere. The elders are trying to find some kind of old deed to your parents' property so that it can be transferred to Elder Grund. They're talking about your mother's marriage in a week."

The thunderous expression on Josh's usual stoic face stunned me. "It's not going to happen. I know where the guns are kept."

"I do too. Gomer Darken's basement is full of them, but we can't blast our way out of here. We have to be clever, Josh. Magdalene Grund told me she has something for me; she said it's a way out."

The angry expression on Josh's face turned to disbelief.

"Sometimes Magdalene says unbelievable things, Jenny. Don't get me wrong. I really like her. She's very knowledgeable about literature and music. I used to play her Steinway. We had some good talks. Zany, unexpected things come out of her mouth. Comes of being a prisoner here." He tugged on the horse's halter to calm it.

"I'm meeting her tonight at the bottom of her hill. I have to take a chance that she can help."

Josh stepped away from me as he eyed Bonita who seemed to be doing some kind of maneuver by the barn—as though she were a World War II flagman who had forgotten the signals. "I don't see anyone, but Bonita is acting strange."

"I think that's her idea of a damsel in distress signal. I'm using her for cover tonight, Josh. I need to get out of your mother's house without being seen so I can meet Magdalene. If you can be on the path to the Grund house by that old fallen fir tree, I'll bring Bonita."

Blood drained out of his face as he let fly a mouthful of words that would bring on Marybeth with her Lifebuoy soap mouthwash: "Why in the fuck would I want to meet that ninny?"

In the distance, I could see a truck churning up clouds of dust behind it. Time was running out.

"Because, Bonita has been assigned by Marybeth to watch me. She can help me get out of the house tonight, but only if she has a compelling reason. You have to be that reason." I turned and stalked off.

I might be a lowlife under stressful circumstances, but I'm not such a sleazebag that I would betray someone as smitten as Bonita. Josh could draw his own conclusions about her feelings. He already had if the ashen hue of his face was any indication of his passion. I was immensely reassured.

I thought about those best friends—the rugged, suave Heathcliff on one string and the golden, godlike Josh on the other. I seemed to be tugging at both of them like an old-fashioned button whirligig.

As I approached Bonita with a big smile, my thought processes would have made the duplicitous Iago blush with shame. Bonita, with all her hand wringing, made a perfect foil. She was addled at the sight of Josh. I would mention his impressive abs later to prime Bonita.

She would probably tell Marybeth everything we talked about today to reassure her that her snooper was on point.

What Bonita would never divulge was any scheme to alert Marybeth that a replacement for Zeb McAfee was as near as the prison for SYM.

NO ONE COULD turn an ordinary, two-story house into a prison faster than Marybeth. She locked the door behind us the minute we stepped from the back porch into the kitchen and pointed to plates with a hunk of stale bread and a slice of rat cheese.

"When I say one hour, that's what I mean. Not ten minutes over. You missed my egg salad for lunch. I'll be keeping my eye on both of you. You won't stir out of this house again without my say-so." She pulled a rocking chair to the center of the kitchen, plopped into it, and pushed herself back and forth, glaring at us.

Bonita sniffled like a kindergarten child sent to a corner

chair. I praised Marybeth for being a disciple of Jeremy Bentham.

"Jeremy who? Jesus had disciples, you wicked girl. Not one of them was called Jeremy. Bonita. Name them for Miss Jenny-know-it-all!"

Before the compliant Bonita had made it past "James son of Zebedee" and headed for John, I shouted: "Enough!" and shoved away cheese fit only for a rat trap.

"I'm talking about the Eighteenth Century philosopher who designed the Panopticon—the prototype for modern prisons—a big circle for the cells and Javert at the center." I smiled archly at Marybeth who rocked as purposelessly as though she might be pumping bilge out of a sinking ship.

"I know that movie! Robert Newton played the police officer who won't give Jean Valjean any peace. Chases him down wherever he tries to go just for stealing a loaf of bread." Bonita got Robert Newton right, but mangled Jean Valjean past recognition.

Bonita cast a guilty look in Marybeth's direction and added apologetically, "An old black and white movie, Marybeth. Pa has a box of them on VHS tapes he got for a bargain. Not TV. We don't watch TV."

"What you do, Bonita, is run them yellow sheets through a tub of bluing, then get them on the line while the sun is still out. And don't waste that cheese."

Like the Pied Piper of Hamlin, Marybeth picked up both pieces of cheese, wrapped them in wax paper and tucked them in her apron pocket—for rat bait or to tempt small children away.

"A one-armed girl is as useless as a one-legged chicken.

Good only for the stew pot," Marybeth sneered at me. "Get over there and stir that good vegetable stew I'm cooking for me and Mr. Darken for supper. At least, you can do that."

She pushed herself up and headed toward the laundry room where Bonita seemed to be making too much noise dipping sheets. "Keep it moving. Don't let it stick. Gomer's not been regular lately. Maylene's cooking, I reckon."

I preferred not to "reckon" as I stirred a motley collection of potatoes, carrots, turnips and something that looked oddly like the kiwis Mother used to put on her face as a restorative mask.

The notion came to me as I *moved* the turgid mass in its pot over a gas burner.

Wild senna. Mrs. Barnes had pointed it out to me as we walked back from the Grund house—or I should think of it as Magdalene's house. Her great grandfather built it. Her father owned it. She was an only child; by rights it should belong to her.

Wild senna—*Senna hebecarpa*—the leaves and pods could be used as a laxative. Mrs. Barnes told me that she collected all kinds of plants—for medicinal uses as well as for their color. She was always trying out different kinds of dyes in her pottery glazes.

"I'm turning down the fire so your stew can simmer, Marybeth," I shouted to no one in particular. "I promised to help Mrs. Barnes with her pottery."

Small glass bottles with carefully lettered labels lined shelf after shelf of a wooden cabinet just inside the pottery shed. Between sassafras and soapwart root was senna.

"Can I help you, Jenny?" Mrs. Barnes smiled at me

warmly, as though I had just walked into her store to browse, not to pilfer. The bottle was tucked into the pocket of that drab dress she had laid out for me yesterday morning, a dress with lots of pockets. Room for knives and guns if any came my way.

"Don't eat the stew," I hissed at her.

"I wouldn't dream of it," she smiled back. "Kale, collards, and turnip greens can be delicious, but not cooked into a pulp with leftovers."

She lifted each bowl drying on a shelf, checking it for flaws. "Might add a little more salt, Jenny. Hides a bitter taste." She turned back to her bowls as though to leave me to my own devices.

Half the bottle should do it with a teaspoon of salt. I stirred the viscous mass vigorously, mildly disappointed that Marybeth would be taking the stew to dine with Mr. Darken at his house, causing me to miss the fireworks—or eruptions.

"YOU AND BONITA will be in bed before Mr. Darken comes by to pick me up. Don't pester Mrs. Barnes. She's got to go through every box in her attic tonight to look for some . . ." Marybeth paused, eyeing us warily, "some church papers."

Marybeth didn't make a good liar. Her nose lifted and twitched like a llama's scenting danger. Church papers, my ass. Someone was putting pressure on Josh's mother to find a missing deed to her property.

Mrs. Barnes seemed fixated on a delicate piece of

greenware on which she was etching flowers. I had the feeling that she wasn't about to comply with Marybeth's demands, considering her reaction after Elder Grund had grabbed her thigh during his therapy.

Creepy old bigot with his rummaging hands. I could just imagine him tying his young wife Magdalene down so he could find out what was hidden in her shoe.

I recalled the suppressed glee in Griselda Grund's voice as she related the terms of Magdalene's marriage contract to Cyrus Grund: "Boot stays on when everything else comes off unless she says different."

An image of a much younger Magdalene, with an oddly made, wide leather boot popped into my mind, like one of those paintings of abducted Sabine women more frightened of what might happen than what was happening at the moment.

Cyrus had exposed Magdalene's deformity. He had taken another wife and moved her into Magdalene's house. If he had remained silent, Magdalene might have been spared madness. She might still be charging up and down the mountainside on a fine horse.

Magdalene might be past saving. Helen Barnes was not. When I managed to get Mother and Lorena out of this hornet's nest, I'd be absolutely certain that Helen Barnes and her son traveled with us.

CHAPTER 9

Traveling anywhere tonight would be problematic. A man I didn't recognize hopped out of Mr. Darken's pickup when he pulled in front of the house, honking rudely. (He no longer drove his wife-baiting Chrysler—I had last seen that car in the possession of Ebon Riley on the Reservation and was highly suspicious of why Ebon had traded it for his pickup just about the time Sue Ann Snelling met death disguised as a car bumper on a deserted road.)

I should go outside and check the bumper for dents, strands of raven hair, pieces of a jingle-jangle dress. I didn't like Sue Ann, but she was a marvel dancing in her leather and quills and beads under a canopy of stars that night on the Reservation. I doubted that the Tribal Police had solved the crime. Somehow Gomer Darken was involved. Ebon Riley certainly was.

"The least you could do is hold the door open for me! This pot is hot. Didn't your mother teach you any manners." It wasn't a question. It was an indictment.

I swung the front door wide with my good arm and did a squat-legged curtsy as vulgar as I could manage. "Good manners are made up of petty sacrifices. Emerson, in case you haven't read him, Marybeth. So sorry to be sacrificing your stew. You and Mr. Darken enjoy."

The hand that yanked me back inside the door was anything but mannerly. Mrs. Barnes flushed with annoyance. "You're not tempting fate, Jenny. You are guaranteeing it. Marybeth and Gomer are vengeful people. It doesn't do to cross them."

I didn't like this conversation. I delighted in crossing them. So, I changed the subject and pointed to the man on the porch who had come with Mr. Darken. "Who's he? The Secret Sharer?"

"That's a man Elder Grund hired to do some yard work for me. I didn't ask for him. Josh has always taken care of our yard, but he hadn't been near this place for a month until he carried you with your dislocated shoulder into the house."

She looked so sad, so wistful that I'd almost dislocate the other shoulder if I could bring her son home. Time for a subject change again. "But, why is that man here so late? It's almost sundown."

"Time for a watcher, a fly on the outside wall. Someone is always here—Marybeth or her stand-in. Elder Grund pays Marybeth to help me, says it's recompense for his therapy, but we know better."

We could hear Bonita humming something in the kitchen that sounded like a dirge. "Marybeth doesn't trust Bonita to be her spy. Poor girl. She was sent here by her tyrant of a father simply for doing what young girls do— talk to boys. Zeb McAfee is a nice boy. She could do worse."

Or better, I thought. *Bonita was going to help me get out of this house tonight to meet with Magdalene Grund, and Josh Barnes would be the decoy.*

"I asked Bonita to whip us up something simple for dinner, an omelet. She'll be busy for now. I want to show you my files that you so generously offered to help organize." If I didn't know Josh's mother to be such a warm, caring person, I might have detected something a bit calculating in her statement.

We walked down the hall to a room on the backside of the house. The view framed by a large double window appeared to be the same pinnacle, from a different angle, where the Grund house perched.

"Isn't that where . . ." I stopped, disoriented for a moment. When we had walked to Magdalene's house, we left by the front door, walked to the north, and cut back no more than half a mile to the east before starting the climb.

"Yes. You're looking at one side of that big hill where the Grund house sits. Two large geological faults run through this area. In the 1880s, miles of lead and silver mines were carved into the surrounding countryside. We were a farming community. Our land was never mined, but the old workings occasionally crossed property lines."

She shoved up one of the sliding windows. "It's stuffy in here. We'll leave this open. We could have taken the back trail to the Grund house, but it's a bit longer. From here, you can see the path just beyond the field winding along the base of the hill."

Clear as a beacon and a window that a girl with a stiff shoulder could hop through with little difficulty.

"Now for my files. It doesn't take that long to make an omelet. Bonita might pop in at any minute. She never knocks. Tutored by Marybeth, I suppose. Can't blame the girl."

I could, but I was breathless. I'd never seen a more orderly office. Plastic bins held tidy stacks. Dozens of binders with clearly identifiable labels lined bookshelves. Not a single sheet of paper appeared to be out of place.

Mrs. Barnes sunk into a leather chair in front of a huge roll top desk, one of those things with a creaky slatted cover. She shoved it up.

I peered over her back, feeling the kind of indefinable pleasure that comes with snooping, reading over someone's shoulder, unlocking a diary that belongs to another, rifling through a stranger's belongings.

A nest of small drawers lined the top of the desk. Mrs. Barnes pulled out each one to show me how cleverly they fit the space with the bottom row jutting out past the upper rows; then, she lifted out one drawer, poked her fingers into the open space, extracted a small cardboard tube, and shook out the contents.

The yellowed sheet of parchment was embossed with seals and half a dozen signatures.

"Magdalene's great grandfather drew up all the documents for the first settlers. By the mid Nineteenth Century, no one used parchment for legal documents, but he did. Made what he called 'fair divisions' with him taking the best. My great-great grandfather owned hundreds of acres, most of what is now considered common land—or taken over by a couple of the elders. Not legal," she added.

She rolled the parchment carefully, shoved it back into the tube, and poked it behind the lower row of small drawers.

"When we go, Jenny. If we go." The pain on her face was tangible. "This has to go with us. Josh knows where I keep it. Some of the elders are very threatened by the information on that deed. They might go to any length to get it, including using me as a pawn."

Remembering the fury on Josh's face when I mentioned that the celestial wedding date of his mother and Elder Grund was drawing near, I wanted to shout at Helen Barnes: "They already are!"

"Omelet's all puffy! Come get it." Bonita sounded as excited as though she had mastered Marybeth's egg salad recipe.

If culinary skills are passed along genetically, Bonita shared a helix with Marybeth. Her idea of "puffy" was a sadly overcooked slab of eggs spruced up with a garnish of parsley. Her notion of dinner conversation was to pry.

"I heard that sometimes Josh plays the piano in church. That must make you real proud, Mrs. Barnes." Bonita doused her omelet with catsup and swirled it around on her plate. "He looks a lot like you, but masculine, you know."

With catsup coating her front teeth, Bonita flashed a vampire smile. I could almost hear the cogs in her empty noggin clicking away, remembering the shirtless Josh.

"I'm crazy about piano music. My pa has a nice collection of old vinyl records—classical stuff like Beethoven and Lawrence Welk. A real treat. I'd love for Josh to listen to them sometime."

My marmoreal face couldn't stay frozen so I complimented

the cook. "Tasty omelet, Bonita." It wasn't a lie. Tasty could mean distinctive. It was that all right.

Bonita seemed a guileless kind of creature, bent on pleasing others, and painfully oblivious that she was coming into estrus over her omelet.

"I thought Josh might be interested in a city girl like Jenny, but Marybeth told me she's bespoken to Jerry Winner or maybe Enoch Bonner. Mr. Darken can't quite decide which one."

Just when I was feeling a bit companionable toward Bonita, I wanted to brain her every other time she opened her mouth.

I wasn't asking for some higher order to weigh the scales in my behalf. I just wanted to sponge away the slime of Gomer Darken from my family. To never again remember him fondling Lorena/Lolita. To never again recall my mother simpering at him from across the table.

I glared across *this* table at Bonita, furious that she had mentioned Mr. Darken. He had debased my family—and my father's memory. "If no one minds, I'm going to bed early. My shoulder aches."

As I headed up the stairs to my bedroom, I glanced out the front window. The guard appeared to be propped up for the night on the porch swing, perched like a cuckoo in a clock, waiting for a puff of air to stir him into action.

Bonita's raspy whisper from the kitchen echoed down the hall. "I didn't mean to make Jenny mad. Either Jerry or Enoch would be a good catch. Pa wants me to marry a man with . . . bald . . . he already has . . . but I'm pretty . . . I shouldn't have . . ."

I couldn't hear anything but a brief, soothing response from Mrs. Barnes and then the soft sound of sobbing.

Like the beaked-nosed Savonarola searching out sinful items for his bonfire of vanities, I sped up the stairs, determined to use the gullible Bonita to keep my rendezvous tonight with Magdalene Grund.

BONITA HAD MASTERED the art of sniveling. She wasn't as loud as the cicadas outside my bedroom window. As she crept into the room, I thought about the life cycle of cicadas, how they live underground as nymphs for seventeen years, then burst into song, sexual frenzy, and bouts of egg laying for only a month or so before their life cycle is complete.

Bonita wouldn't be allowed to sprout wings. She'd be forced to crawl grub-like into the bed of a man she detested and live out her days pretending that Lawrence Welk was a "real treat."

"Sit by me on the bed, Bonita. Let's get better acquainted." I patted the bed, wondering if my nose was humping worse than Savonarola's. "I'm going to help you spend some quality time with Josh tonight—if you want to." I forced a note of casualness, as if I were describing a well-supervised church picnic.

"There's a guard on the front porch, if you haven't noticed," Bonita retorted acidly.

"I have. But I know a way out so he can't see us. And if he does, we're just going for a little walk on a starry, starry night." I couldn't seem to get Don McLean's "Vincent" out of my mind. "How you suffered for your sanity" had become my mantra in this weird place.

The entire day had a gray, scoured feel about it. No ripples of light filtered through low-hanging clouds, but the night sky gloried in layer after layer of stars.

The anticipation of "quality time" with Josh—whatever that might mean to Bonita—had stifled her sniffling and promoted as much of an adventurous spirit as I could expect from someone who thought of Lawrence Welk as entertainment.

Minutes later, we were down the stairs, inside the office and out the back window. A flashlight had miraculously appeared on the windowsill.

Skirting a coop of startled hens, we cut through the back herb garden, scooted under the fence and took a cow path toward the bluff where a back trail supposedly led onto the path going up the forested bluff to Magdalene's house.

I dared not turn on the flashlight until we were well out of sight of the Barnes's house, but under the gibbous moon, we could just make out the narrow path.

And something long wiggling across it. In spite of my hand clamped over her shrieking mouth, Bonita churned her legs and threshed against me wildly, struggling to flee. Pain shot through my splinted shoulder as I toppled her to the ground.

"Bonita, you dumb shit. That was a harmless grass snake. There are no venomous snakes around here," I hissed. For a girl with a decent vocabulary, I seemed to regress to grade school taunts around Bonita.

"I thought it might be a rattlesnake. Pa says that girls

can't wander off at night, because they have a scent that particularly attracts rattlesnakes. That's how the snake in the Garden of Eden found Eve. Rattlesnakes are thick as thieves around Boise. Pa says so." Her voice was thick with reproach.

So that's how the saints keep their daughters from a little night music. Eve and her attraction to a snake was a mythology the CPRC bunch used to keep the girls in the henhouse.

"That's utter nonsense, Bonita. Snakes can sense thermal radiation—the heat of their prey. That's how they find food. Unless girls get hotter than boys, it's unlikely they'll attract snakes more quickly."

That thought prompted an entire biology lesson that Bonita might find useful, but lying in tall grass in the middle of a pasture at night didn't seem to be the right venue for her education.

Except for a chorus of frogs croaking around a nearby pond, no one seemed disturbed by Bonita's shriek. I started to make a wide berth around the pond—the one where Abigail floated in a watery grave after Jerry snapped her neck.

"This is where they found Abigail, isn't it?" Bonita's whisper sounded harsh, too curious about my dead friend who was also a friend of Zeb MacAfee.

I ignored her and continued to angle far past the edge of the pond.

"I heard talk that her mama didn't think she would drown herself. Said she couldn't swim and was afraid of deep water. Said someone might have done it."

I knew exactly who had done it. Jerry Winner with his knee-high boots and Hitler mustache still walked the planet as though assured that the Third Reich never lost the war. Sharing that information with Bonita would be a bad mistake. She needed to think I was playing off Jerry and Enoch against each other—leaving the field clear for her to pursue Josh.

"My old gran on Pa's side said that if someone is suspected of murder that person could be made to touch the corpse. If they're guilty, fresh blood will gush out of the corpse. And Bob's your uncle; you have the killer. Gran says Bob's your uncle all the time. Her ma came from Liverpool in England."

While I was getting this bit of family history and learning new crime detection methods, I couldn't help thinking about the "mush wouldn't melt in her mouth" comment about Abigail that Bonita had made when I first met her. At the moment, I was wishing I'd done more damage to Bonita when I pulled her down. My shoulder throbbed with enough pain for both of us.

High on the hill above us I could see the outline of Magdalene's house like a sketch by Gorey, sinister with unseen goblins.

I flicked on the flashlight. Just ahead of us the path forked. The more worn path was the one that Griselda, Mrs. Barnes and I had taken the day before. I decided to take Frost's advice.

"The one less traveled by. Go to the right, Bonita."

"And that has made all the difference." The amused voice of Josh Barnes came softly from behind an enormous fir. "Evening, ladies. Fancy meeting you here." He pulled off a baseball cap with an odd phallic design on it and swooped a low bow.

I aimed my flashlight at him. The cap he dangled from his forefinger had a rough outline of the state of Idaho on it.

I shone the flashlight on the large fallen fir where I had been sitting the day before comforting Josh's mother. It was thick, mossy and rounded—just uncomfortable enough to keep a couple upright and focused on balance rather than sex.

"Why don't you two sit and visit while I go on up this other path? There's a good vantage point forty feet or so up the main path. I'll keep watch."

Like a docile, well-trained animal, Josh sat on the spot I patted. Bonita squished in closer than she needed to. "Your mama told me you play the piano. I absolutely love the piano. Jo Ann Castle plays a honky-tonk piano on Lawrence Welk. She's really good. I'll bet you are too." The damp, mossy log against her rump wasn't cooling Bonita.

I dared not look at Josh's face. His limbs had gone stiff as though rigor mortis was setting in. "Don't be gone long, Jenny. We don't know who might be prowling around." The tension in his voice was palpable.

Chapter 10

The person prowling around was Magdalene. Wearing a black flowing cloak like something the Scarlet Pimpernel would have worn to hide from Madame Defarge, Magdalene floated toward me on the main path. In the darkness, her haunted eyes glistened.

As I walked closer, I could see that under the waves of black satin, she was wearing virginal white, a diaphanous Greek-style gown. Her body was slim, girlish. She smiled a gap-toothed grin. With new dentures, she'd be an attractive old woman.

"Clever of you to set Josh up as a decoy."

"I wasn't . . . I didn't . . ." I stared into eyes whose cataract glaze lent them an odd opaque quality and decided to be truthful.

"I needed Bonita to come along. She sleeps in my room and would have blown the whistle if I left without her. She's attracted to Josh. I just made the best of an opportunity—and Josh agreed. Reluctantly. We probably don't have much time."

Magdalene nodded and held out a large rectangular object wrapped in dark cloth. "Keys to the kingdom."

Her cackle might have come from a crow.

What was I doing with a madwoman in the night?

"Tunnel vision is what keeps us from finding the tunnel." Her voice softened as she enunciated each word carefully and stepped on a flat rock next to the path as though she were standing on the edge of a stage ready to perform.

"The Liberty we knew
Avoided—like a dream
Too wide for any Night but Heaven—
If that—indeed—redeem."

Magdalene bowed toward me with a quizzical look. "Maylene told me you know our best poets. Surely you ..."

"Know Emily? A prison gets to be a friend? Yes. It's not my favorite poem lately." I returned her bow with a curt nod. Playing name the author with a deranged woman in a primeval forest at midnight seemed almost sporting under the circumstances.

I stepped toward her, eased out my hand with glacial slowness, and took the parcel. It might hold coils of asps. It's at times like this that you find out if you're made of what they call "sterner stuff."

At the moment I felt suffused in cowardly yellow. I wanted to run. I wanted to snatch Bonita out of Josh's arms—where she must be nestled at this moment—and wrap myself like a boa around him.

"Just checking to be sure you aren't neglecting the women poets. Helen says you have a mathematical mind. So did my great-grandfather. Skipped the next generations." She reached over to lightly caress the bundle I was holding. "These are Daniel Marchman's journals—all his records from his trip west. There are pages filled with his survey information—surface details as well as geological all the way to the Bitterroot Range. I still have the transit and theodolite he used for horizontal and vertical angles."

My ears perked up. Magdalene's great-grandfather and I might have had some fine discussions about angles.

"I put his smaller brass compass in the bundle. You might need it. My great-grandfather's journal is full of details about the problems with Flatheads, Nez Perce and Blackfoot tribes. That might not seem to be of much interest, but it led to them searching for a hidden way out of here. The reason the entrance and exit were kept secret and then passed to the senior elder is pure speculation. He doesn't say."

She tapped long witchy fingers with impossibly scarlet nails on the box. "In big letters at the beginning of the section on the tunnel, he wrote: 'think of a Platonic solid.' I don't have the foggiest about what he meant." She smiled winsomely at me. "I'd give a decade of my life to know."

"Geometric figures—regular, convex polyhedrons with congruent faces. Tetrahedrons, cubes, octahedrons, dodecahedrons, and icosahedrons." My schoolmarm's voice irritated even me.

"Yes, dear. I know what Euclid meant, but I don't know what any of that has to do with the layout or location of a tunnel leading out of this place—a tunnel that might have stored items for a quick escape."

Magdalene's voice reminded me faintly of Mother's when I got too prissy for my own good.

"Later, when the miners arrived, our people chased

them off our land, but their old mine workings might extend under parts of our property. Our family would never have agreed to the savaging of the underground."

She cackled again as though struck by something amusing. "Francis Bacon said that important families are like potatoes—the best parts are underground."

Though I was fond enough of Bacon's inductive methods, I put on my soberest face to temper the direction Magdalene's conversation seemed to be going. A bone-chilling dampness settled around us.

Magdalene sunk down with surprising agility for someone who seemed so aged. "Sit close by me on this good earth, Jenny. We may not have another opportunity to talk, so we need to make the most of our time."

Balancing myself on my one good arm, I sat at a safe distance, crossing my legs yoga style. Magdalene patted the ground next to her; I moved closer, so close I could see her breath making little vaporous puffs in the night chill.

"We were the wealthiest family in the Compound, but all I ever wanted from this life was to wake up every morning loving this land my great-grandfather found or stole from the Indians, although he considered them Lamanites, one of the lost tribes of Israel. We Marchmans never had a honed sense of guilt." Magdalene sniffed the night air as though she might have smelled rue.

"I knew I could bring shame upon my parents because of my deformity." She shoved one foot with an odd, squared-off boot out from under her.

"I grew up avoiding other people, riding my horses from one end of this land to the other. I have never been as much outside of myself as I wanted to be for fear that someone would know what my parents kept hidden." She pulled her booted foot under her skirt.

"When I reached the marriageable age, my father worried because I had no siblings or aunts and uncles to look after me." She smiled that ragged-toothed smile that looked almost charming in the moonlight.

"I had plenty of men wanting to look after me—look after my property is what they wanted. Like beetles out of rotting wood, they came to court me from compounds all over the region. My father was suspicious of their intentions. Damn and blast, Papa, I said to him. Pick someone here. A known commodity."

She closed her eyes and lifted her face silently to the moon like a wolf too forlorn to howl.

"So, he picked Cyrus Grund. Cyrus was twenty-five, six years older than me, a church-going, hard-working man. He was intimidated by my father and by our wealth. My father thought he would keep the agreement."

She shoved herself backward, stretched her booted foot and said softly. "The day after my father died, Cyrus took off my shoe, knocked out two of my teeth, and sold my horses."

Magdalene scooted closer to me until our knees were touching. "The most important thing tucked inside these journals is the deed to my property. I've hidden it all these years from Cyrus. Cost me two more teeth, but worth it."

"But, I don't know what . . ."

"My handwritten will is there with the deed. Witnessed by those men Cyrus hired to keep me from disappearing.

They despise that old fool." She gripped my hand.

"Everything goes to you and Josh. Together. Or split down the middle. Except he gets the Steinway. Josh doesn't know. It's our secret, Jenny, because you are the girl I once was and lost."

The look she gave me was so full of simple, uncomplicated affection that I forgot she might be more than half mad. Then, tears dripped silently down her old cheeks like molten silver in the moonlight.

The oddest feeling came over me, as though I were watching a young child in great need of comfort. I pulled her close to me and murmured: "Hush. Hush, my dear, I have come to help you."

She pushed herself back slowly with a heartfelt look, as though I'd just dropped an intimate love sonnet on her.

"The last person to call me 'my dear' was Papa on his deathbed. I knew we would be best friends, Jenny. I knew from the gossip about your tricks with electricity and the way you set Gomer Darken on edge that we had a live one amongst us."

She fumbled around in the pocket of her cloak and drew out a fist-sized chocolate colored rock.

"One more thing you might need. This is your seer stone."

"My what?"

"Seer stone. For see-er. Every person born has a seer stone; most of them never know it. Joseph Smith could find anything with his. The stones helped him translate the golden plates. Or Urim and Thummim helped translate. It's one of our mysteries, Jenny. Has to do with angels."

She closed my fist around the smooth stone.

"Somehow, our people lost the knack of finding treasures with their stones. This one belonged to my great-grandfather. He found two water wells. Lots of other things. Never did find his lost pocket watch. I'm hoping it will help you find your way out of here."

The sounds of Bonita and Josh coming up the path startled me into action. With considerable pain, I pushed Magdalene's bundle under my sling, zipped up my hoodie, and tucked the stone into my pocket.

Then, I put one arm around her and kissed a tissue-like cheek that smelled of lemon verbena and uttered words as solemn as any oath I would ever take: "We *are* best friends, Magdalene Marchman. Best friends forever. I will find a way. I will."

By the time Josh and Bonita appeared on the path below, Magdalene had vanished. Josh took off in the opposite direction without a word. The cicadas sang even louder.

Something at the very core of my being had quickened and changed. A very strange old woman had given me the best gift imaginable—irrefutable trust.

LIKE THE CHURRING call of a nightjar, the continuous rattling of Bonita's voice covered everything from an engagement and a wedding to how many children she and Josh might produce if her father could just be brought to heel.

Shushing her as regularly as a librarian, I asked only one question: "So Josh proposed to you?"

The chattering stopped for a moment as we rounded the pond. "No, silly. We don't do it that way around here. The boy has to go to the girl's father first. Josh wouldn't dare be so disrespectful," she retorted and flounced on ahead of me.

"Then how do you . . ." I was almost afraid to ask for fear I'd get a graphic description of the sexual act atop a fallen log.

"You just know. Josh asked me all kinds of questions, especially about those VHS tapes Pa lets us watch. He said he liked Mr. Bogart. He didn't seem to know much about the movies I like, so I talked about Doris Day. He mostly listened. I could tell he really likes me. He was so quiet, almost spellbound," she giggled.

More like in a coma, I thought. I wouldn't dissuade Bonita from following where her heart seemed to be leading her. Our little secret meant that she had to trust me. I could use that trust to my advantage.

As we skirted the hencoop from some distance, a great flutter and squawking split the silence of the night. Bonita grabbed my right arm and raced me toward the back of Mrs. Barnes's house where we crouched under the open window. "Fox or coyote," she hissed. "He'll be here in a second."

A shadowy figure strode past us with a beam aimed at the hencoop as my heart pounded like a Sousa march. The watcher waved his flashlight across the hexagons of chicken wire, checking for damage, muttered something and retraced his steps.

Within seconds, Bonita was pushing me up through the

window. In addition to a dislocated shoulder to maneuver through the window, I needed to keep Magdalene's bundle hidden beneath my sling.

I scrabbled up the side of the house, using my good arm to keep my disabled shoulder from touching the window frame as I plopped like a beached seal onto the floor of the study.

Feigning intense pain, I whispered: "You go ahead, Bonita. Be sure the coast is clear. I'll come up to bed in a few minutes. I need to relax. Spasms in my shoulder."

When I heard her reach the top step, I eased Magdalene's bundle from underneath my sling, lifted out two leather-bound books, and shoved the sheets of loose parchment into one of them.

Not daring to turn on a flashlight, I groped my way past the desk over to the wall with bookcases. Walking my fingers along the shelves, I found an open space and shoved in Daniel Marchman's journals. Marybeth would be sure to check under my mattress. She'd never look at a bookshelf.

The small brass compass glinted in the light of a waning moon. I shoved it in one of my pockets and folded up the cloth that wrapped the books. The piece of cloth had several metallic bands along the edge of it, but I had no time to examine it now. I stuffed it in my pocket and slipped through the door.

The nightlight by the front door cast enough of a glow for me to see the Waterbury mantle clock on a side table by the staircase. Two o'clock. This kind of Waterbury was not my favorite clock—a bit too much wood décor unbalanced it, but the 1880s clock appeared to be in good condition.

I'd offer to clean it. Take it apart in Mrs. Barnes's office. Leave parts all over the floor so no one could come in the room. With only one working arm, it would take me a long time. Time that I would need to be alone with the intricate workings of a clock's innards. Enough time to examine some old leather-bound books.

CHAPTER 11

There was no need to explain the evening outing to Mrs. Barnes when I surfaced the next morning. She had spotted the mud and fir needles on the tennis shoes I left on the floor in her office when I came through the window; she dangled their clean soles in front of me.

"Marybeth hasn't quite recovered from a bad night of what she says is flu, so she may not be here today. Ordinarily, she arrives early and starts the day by saying that she doesn't find it the least bit funny that her waxed floors get dirty—even when they don't," Mrs. Barnes said in an exasperated tone.

"It's hard to be funny when you have to be clean. Mae West said that." I grabbed my tennis shoes and bent over to stuff my feet in them while peering slyly up at Helen Barnes to see if she picked up on the double entendre. She had. The tiniest smile flitted around the corners of her mouth.

"Bonita was snoring like a hibernating bear when I left the bedroom. We had a little walk up the hill last night." I wasn't going to lie to Mrs. Barnes. I just wasn't going to tell her everything. The elders might resort to torture, so my plans needed to stay inside my head.

"Yes. Josh climbed the wisteria outside my bedroom window very early this morning to let me know you and Bonita were back safely."

"But, I thought that Magdalene and I had ..." I stuttered.

"Secrets? You do. I saw Magdalene whispering to you on the porch after she had done her best to distract Griselda by shocking the hired help. I made a special point of taking her some herbal tea to calm her down before I finished Cyrus's therapy session. She told me she was giving you her great-grandfather's journals."

"Anything else?" *Magdalene had been emphatic about no one else knowing about her will.*

"No. She did say that you reminded her of herself as a girl and that she wanted better lives for you and Josh." Mrs. Barnes frowned slightly. "Perched up on that big four-poster bed of hers, she seemed to be bestowing a kind of blessing on both of you as she tossed that old seer stone of her father's from one hand to the other. She said she had given her great-grandfather's seer stone away."

Mrs. Barnes glanced out the front hall window. The watcher was still there, chopping away at nonexistent weeds around the porch. She took my hand and headed toward the office. "You can study those old journals in here, Jenny. I'll bring you some breakfast."

"And your Waterbury clock," I added.

"My clock? It's ..."

"In dire need of cleaning. I'm very good with clocks. Trust me. When I'm working on it, the movement pieces will be disassembled and scattered strategically all across the floor. Marybeth won't dare to make a surprise visit."

Without a word, Mrs. Graves lifted her antique clock and carried it down the hall to the office. I hurried along behind her, eager to get those journals into the light of day.

DANIEL MARCHMAN'S FIRST journal might as well have stayed on the shelf for all the clues to a secret tunnel it provided.

Stained and travel-worn, the first journal was an account of the daily trials of traveling with women and children in wagons packed to excess with what the new settlers thought they would need—prized household goods that caused the oxen to strain against the load and the wagon wheels to sink.

No less than eight miles east of the Great Salt Lake, my first-born son Caleb was stricken from this life after a misadventure with a great grizzly. Two haunches of fresh venison strapped to his mule attracted the beast. Had I known the danger, I would have starved.

I intended to camp overnight and hold a service for my dear son before we trekked on to Fort Buenaventura, but the guide warned us that hostiles were in the area. So, we wrapped Caleb in his mother's fine shawl and tucked him under a rock slide. Not five miles behind, we had left his mother's Regency wardrobe beside the trail. She started grieving then and can't seem to quiet her sobs. I promised to grasp the hand of Providence and return for our son and her mahogany cabinet when we are well-placed in the land of promise.

His wife's concern that her Regency wardrobe had to be left by the trail seemed to trouble Mr. Marchman almost as much as his oldest son's run in with a grizzly.

The little map in the journal struck me as more poignant than the words that were not written. Daniel Marchman had carefully struck the longitude and latitude of where he had left his wife's Regency wardrobe and where he had buried their son.

Almost every new entry identified the "land of promise" ahead and the "hand of providence" guiding them. I got the distinct feeling that Daniel Marchman with his compass, transit, theodolite and "chain with 100 links" considered his hand closely linked to that of Providence.

The man spoke my language and saw things with my eyes. Every range of mountains was an "infinite variation of triangles." Vast, rolling plains were cordoned off into "geometric" patterns.

When Daniel Marchman linked the Fibonacci sequence to the branching of trees, the leaves on a stem, and the precise way a fern uncurls so magically and numerically perfect, I knew that he and I were on the same wavelength. If the secret to a tunnel had been left as a cipher, I would find it.

On to the second journal. This book began with a brief postlude about the parting with Brigham Young at the Great Salt Lake Valley. Unstained by the rigors of travel, the second journal was in pristine condition. Mr. Marchman described the claim cabins built by his people for shelter and the way he had marked off 640 acres for the initial compound with his cabin at the uppermost point.

Page after page documented baselines, bearings, conditional lines between properties and landmarks—piles of rocks or groves of trees that probably no longer existed.

Right there in the middle of a page, set out like a multi-faceted diamond in fading brownish ink was a Platonic solid—a hexahedron.

Just below it the text began:

All of our efforts to demonstrate friendship to the Lamanites have been for naught. They covet our tools, our guns, the whiteness of our women. The hides they bring for trade are mangy and stiff with age. We must find a shelter that they cannot torch and with walls they cannot climb.

A month passed before the next entry. It was a sad little note:

Isaiah Felton, his wives Rebecca and Mary, and three children met an untimely end when they ventured out to pick blackberries after prayer service. We think a rogue band of Shoshone came upon them. The grizzly that took my son offered him a kinder end. I cannot speak of that butchery without weeping like a woman.

The margins around the next note contained tiny sketches of polyhedrons done in pencil with nice shadings to highlight their dimensionality. The text said:

"My small daughter Magdalene has found a place to sequester ourselves from savage assaults. The wild honeybees swarm near. That child is a gift but born mute as

though God did not want her to speak any secrets nor let the devil govern her tongue."

Or, I thought, something happened in the Broca's area of her brain to block speech. Interesting how the saints were always blaming God from the get-go for any infirmities. At least, her father saw it as a blessing of sorts. I thought of this small, silent ancestor of Magdalene Grund and wondered if she might be looking down on her namesake with the maimed foot.

I flipped back to Marchman's sketches of the land his group of settlers had claimed from the Indians. The floor plan of his cabin sat on top of the same bluff where he built his mansion in the 1870s.

If his young, mute daughter had found a hidey-hole, it must be somewhere on or around this bluff. Surely, she wouldn't have been allowed to wander afield.

A few entries later were topped by the words: *"Cave and way out surely designed by the Lord on high."* There was not a single reference, not a solitary drawing that would give any clue to its location.

Along the margins were neat little sketches of polyhedrons, four-sided, six-sided, eight-sided, twelve-sided. Maybe the man just had polyhedrons on the brain, liked drawing them. Perhaps they had nothing to do with a secret tunnel.

But there it was. The tunnel itself. Just a long tube-like sketch branching in all directions with tiny arrows dipping west, then east, to the north, and east again. A sketch of an opening appeared to be covered with a profusion of vines tipped by clusters of flowers.

He had drawn something that looked like a small octopus underground. The marks along a line at the top of the page might have represented meters or kilometers.

As a surveyor, Daniel would have used the metric system. When the Vicar of St. Paul's Cathedral in France determined the meter to be one minute of arc on the surface of the earth in the year 1670, all measurement-minded people on the globe went along with him.

Daniel had probably drawn his underground squiggly lines in centimeters but had given no clue to the conversion factor. I flipped through the rest of the journal but found no other references to a cave or tunnel. I slammed the journal shut with frustration.

The tunnel could be anywhere within this vast wilderness that was claimed by the saints. I wasn't going to find it by sneaking out of captivity occasionally with Bonita trailing along to report back to Marybeth.

"You get yourself out here right now, Jenny Hatchet! Mr. Darken is here to see you." Marybeth's screech preceded a vigorous banging on the office door.

I scooped up the journals and replaced them on the shelves, then spread out the clock's innards so that no one would dare step into the room, and closed the door quietly behind me.

What could that pervert possibly want? The pain that had just begun clenching my stomach made me wonder if the senna laxative I had dumped into Marybeth's stew had made it home to roost. Mrs. Barnes's homemade peanut butter on her own baked bread couldn't be causing my discomfort. The notion that GOD was in the next room did.

Gomer Obadiah Darken sprawled across the best sofa in the parlor and was leaving a sizeable ring with a glass of lemonade on Mrs. Barnes's nice walnut table.

"Jenny, my girl. I came by to check on your shoulder. Your mother worries herself silly about you girls. I do too, of course." Like an unrehearsed scene in a bad melodrama, Mr. Darken groped for his lines.

"Sit down. Sit down." He patted the sofa next to him. His wolfish smile made me wish they'd take wolves off the list of endangered species.

I perched on the edge of a hard-back chair situated as far from the sofa as any chair in the room and gave him my undivided attention, trying to remember all the cursers in the Bible: God cursing the serpent, Noah cursing Canaan, Jesus cursing the fig tree. I lost my train of thought with his next statement.

"We've come to a little impasse." Curious how he stressed the word impasse—as though it had an accent over the "e."

"Two of our finest young men—Jerry and Enoch—have both approached me. Rather, their fathers individually approached me. About your hand."

I lifted a pale, limp hand out of my sling, thinking the CPRC elders must be developing some sense of civility. Probably wanting to apologize for their sons' barbaric treatment of me. About time.

The smugness of my expression encouraged Mr. Darken to confide in me.

"I find myself in a peculiar dilemma beings I made this agreement of sorts with Elder Winner without quite . . .

but it was within my rights . . . well, you know." If sheep-ishness could go hand-in-glove with self-righteousness, Mr. Darken had mastered the trick.

"No. I don't know." I said icily, remembering my week of confinement in an attic with nothing to wear but castoffs of Leah Winner's triple X daughter and nothing to read but the *Book of Mormon* and a Bible.

"It's an honor for a girl without a cent to her name to be pursued by the two most eligible young men in our extended family. But, it comes with a problem." He moved his glass sideways so the puddle it was making would double the destructiveness.

"Your *extended family*," I spat out, "has a screwy notion of honor if they don't consider kidnapping and assault as felonies punishable by jail time—a bit more than a prob-lem, I'd say."

"The *problem*," he carefully ignored my accusations, "is that my promotion comes up at our district council meeting soon. I need two of our three senior elders to recommend me."

He shuffled his feet nervously, like an amateur tap dancer just about to hit the spotlight. "Elder Grund and I struck a deal for a quarter section of his land—takes in that old Indian burial ground just to the side of his house so I got it at a good price—along with Elder Grund's promise to vote me up."

I wanted to ask him how he could possibly strike a deal with Elder Grund about a piece of property that Magdalene owned, but I kept quiet. Gomer Darken was clearly stressed about this promotion thing.

"You see, Jenny. I've been on the list for a promotion for a very long time. I didn't inherit the title the way that Jerry and Enoch as oldest sons will come into their positions. I had to prove myself financially and by my character. The well-being of CPRC rests with its elders."

"And this affects me how?" If tone could etch, Mr. Darken's body would be bloody by now.

"It affects you, young lady, because you've caused a serious riff between Jerry and Enoch. Now that riff extends to their fathers. Elder Grund informs me that if I don't remediate it, I won't be standing as an elder. Elders must be in accord."

Mr. Darken turned his face quickly away from me and seemed to be fascinated by the terminal struggles of a bottle fly on the windowsill. If I didn't know better, I might have seen a single tear sluicing down the side of his face.

Like Phaedrus on the horns of a dilemma, my first retort would have been too obvious: kidnap another fifteen-year-old girl who loves running and tinkering with old clocks and make the boys draw straws.

Sarcasm did not bode well in this situation. Mr. Darken needed my help. I would give it to him.

Like a thunderbolt, a way to search the miles of CPRC holdings came to me. Suppressing a snarky grin, I said with more sincerity than I'd felt for some time. "You need the wisdom of Solomon this time, Mr. Darken. I don't think either of those boys will settle for the top half of a girl."

Just as his head snapped toward me, I cushioned the next blow. "Tell them—no. Tell their fathers that I'm a girl who has to be courted. City girl. Different culture. I like driving around with boys. It will give me a chance to get to know each of them better."

I stuck out my arm in its sling and turned a pitiful face toward my wanna-be stepfather. "I can't defend my honor. One of them tries to cross the line, and he's out as a husband candidate."

The light that came on in Mr. Darken's eyes would compete with a neon sign. "That's really brilliant, Jenny. The boys act like gentlemen, they have a chance with you. They don't, it's their own fault. Their fathers can't blame me if they misbehave. It's the kind of solution worthy of an elder."

Or a girl who needed transportation to every nook and cranny of this godforsaken place.

"You arrange the times with them, Mr. Darken. Not today. I'm helping Mrs. Barnes with her filing. I'm also cleaning her antique clock. Afternoons would be fine."

Like Queen Victoria dispensing the same five pounds to the Battersea Dogs Home as she did to the Irish, I smiled benignly across the room, as though we should have more of these pleasant conversations.

CHAPTER 12

When Jerry Winner whipped a flame-red Dodge Ram 3500 pickup precisely across the end of Mrs. Barnes's stone walkway to keep his shiny boots out of the dirt, I would not have been surprised to see Hitler stepping from his 1935 Mercedes with that odd little twitch of a smile he wore for his speeches about "glorious victories."

His air of possessiveness penetrated into the front parlor where I nervously awaited the first of the two princes of the realm.

Remembering the almost casual ease with which Jerry had sorted out the precise location of my carotid with his burly thumbs in a Spokane alley, I had a feeling that engaging him in small talk about movies or music might be counterproductive.

From the parlor window, I could see him stroking the back fender of his truck, the way a trainer might calm a jittery racehorse. He spit on his right hand and plastered his wayward forelock down, looking at himself in the side mirror.

As he goose-stepped up to the front door, I thought of Noyes's poem "The Highwayman." Jerry was no dashing thief. I was nothing like Bess the landlord's daughter with her perfumed waves of hair. But, I felt a sense of her doom as a fist banged against the door.

Like Cinderella's overbearing stepmother, Marybeth swung the door wide and offered me up as a collateral descendant. "My stepdaughter Jenny is waiting for you to take her for a little spin in that nice new truck of yours, Jerry. Two hours maximum. I'm whipping up a prune cake for a nice snack when you get back."

I smiled as benevolently as though I might have been envisioning orange blossoms atop her prune cake. A strategically dropped slice of Marybeth's prune cake could crush a booted toe.

Boosting a one-armed girl into a pickup that sat a yard high off the ground might have justified a misplaced hand on one boob—not on two. Jerry had all the finesse of a buffalo in rut. I needed to parry with the same subtlety.

"Show me what this monster truck of yours will do, Jerry. I'll bet it can't make it down into the canyon and up the other side where those flat rocks form a kind of ledge." I pointed toward a bluff east of Magdalene's property.

I had spent the morning sectioning off the 640 acres that Daniel Marchman had claimed for the original compound. The trouble with the Indians started with the initial settlement; I was sure that the tunnel would be within the original boundary lines.

I intended to keep Jerry and Enoch traversing the property until I found some likely locations for a more detailed exploration.

With the enthusiasm of a jeep climber approaching

Hells Gate in Moab, Jerry rose to the bait and roared off down one side of the canyon, almost got stuck in the shallow creek, and canted dangerously over the edge of a narrow rock outcropping as I urged him along.

"Pa would skin me alive if he saw me mistreating my truck like this." Perspiration dripped from Jerry's domed forehead as he veered onto a small flat space leading into a forest. He slammed on his brakes and peered across at me with glassy blue eyes.

"Fun, wasn't it?" I patted his arm with the same affection I'd offer to a strange dog that brought back a thrown stick. Indifferently.

"Let's take a breather. I want to walk along that ledge behind us. The view up there was breathtaking." I flung my good arm out to encompass the hodgepodge of compound buildings below. I needed to walk, to get out of the confines of this pickup cab. Adolph was inching too close for comfort.

I shoved open the door, dropped awkwardly to the ground, and headed off toward the ridge at a fast clip. Daniel Marchman talked about "strange sedimentary structures" in his journal. Caves might be found in those kinds of rocks.

Wanting to take a closer look, I ignored Jerry's sharp order to "stay here" and started up a narrow animal trail that led through dense thickets of kinnikinnick. I paused for a moment, thinking of Sue Ann Snelling curled among the glossy leaves and velvety stems of this same plant on the Res.

While out for a morning run with Heathcliff, we had come upon the body of the dancing princess in this same kind of brush at the edge of a fir forest on the Reservation.

I thought instantly of Heath cupping the perfectly formed bare feet of Sue Ann and trembling with emotion too inexplicable for tears.

The steel band posing as an arm crushing my ribs into splinters vied with the lump of a fist pressed against my mouth.

I struggled helplessly, my shoulder fracturing with unbearable pain. Jerry's notion of a good rape scene would have bested a Viking raiding party. Sneak up, grab, demobilize and do the deed.

The odor hit me first—the scent of dried clover. Then the sound—like a shovel being dragged across concrete pavement, as crisp and gravelly as a monster clearing its throat.

The grizzly and her cub were not thirty yards ahead of us. Like a tableau vivant, we were frozen into one of those historical scenes where the worst was going to happen as soon as time defrosted itself.

I couldn't take my eyes off the cub. Its twinkling brown eyes seemed almost mischievous, as though it would welcome a nice tumble with another bear.

The Chimaera of Greek mythology—the she-goat creature who breathed fire—must have been a cousin of this grizzly mother. The flames burning in her eyes seared me from yards away, as though her rage might consume me without engaging tooth or claw.

"Don't move. Don't speak." Jerry hissed into one of my ears as he stepped back carefully, crushing me against him so tightly that I would already be tenderized meat if the bear decided to charge.

With each step backwards, he paused for what seemed an eternity, then took another step.

At that moment, I knew how much could be encapsulated in a second of time: odors of clover and wet grass, eyes flickering blood red, a great hump of fur that encompassed every conceivable maternal instinct and a perspiring male body that would not let me race for my own life.

In that brief moment, I despised Jerry Winner more than I ever had before. While he was holding me in a death grip in front of him as the top patty on the Big Mac, he was preventing me from sprinting away. I knew bears could do 30 miles an hour; I might do 20 under stress. It was worth a try, but I couldn't move.

Then I did. I was no longer plastered against Jerry's sweaty body; his vice-like hands moved me solemnly forward—the way a priest places a wafer representing the body of Christ onto the limp tongue of a kneeling parishioner.

Perhaps it was simply a fluke of the light filtering through the forest, but the flames in the eyes of that grizzly softened to tiny sparks that seemed to glow with solicitude.

With the air of King Kong swatting away a human fly, the huge grizzly snorted once and moved with dirge-like slowness down the trail until she and her cub were out of sight.

"You got a screw loose or something?" Jerry screeched at me. "You don't go running around in this part of the country like that. We're close to Glacier. Grizzlies don't stay in the park!" His screeching had become a frustrating bark, annoying in the extreme.

I stalked back to his pickup, yanked open the door and pulled myself up effortlessly.

When Jerry climbed into the truck, his face was perfectly composed again, with that odd little inch of a mustache clenched into his upper lip. When he lifted his hands to clutch the steering wheel, the dead giveaway of fear pooled in his armpits.

Our little trip to the zoo without bars had scared him shitless. My own armpits were deodorized, fresh as a spring rain—as the bottle I borrowed from Mrs. Barnes attests. I have no idea what that means. Jerry might need something stronger than rain, but I had to make amends. I still needed transportation to explore the Compound.

"You were absolutely fearless, Jerry." I cooed. "So slow. So cautious. So prudent." *Yeah, like someone offering his girlfriend up as the appetizer to a bear ready to charge.*

"*Imprudent*, if the truth be told," he snapped back at me. "Considering your idiotic behavior."

A sour expression drifted across Jerry's face as he fingered the empty gun rack behind his head. "Pa told me to leave my gun at home when I go courting. Bad idea. We heard tell of a grizzly and her cub being spotted near the Grund house just last week."

"What kind of gun?" I asked brightly, hoping to shift the conversation to something less personal than our encounter with a bear and Jerry's sudden interest in my thighs.

Earlier, we had pretty much exhausted the truck as a topic as we chugged up the canyon: three-link front suspension, 383 horsepower at 5600 RPM and something about tires that I didn't get.

"A .338 Winchester Magnum. Pa give it to me for my sixteenth. It's a beaut. A pleasure to use."

"I wouldn't mind learning to shoot your gun, Jerry," I pronounced with considerable enthusiasm at the thought of drilling Mr. Darken pointblank between his eyes.

"Nope. Too powerful. Bam. Knock your other shoulder out of whack. Put you completely at my mercy." He leaned across me and readjusted my seatbelt, fitting the strap neatly between both my nipples that were inverting themselves in silent protest.

"We could let you try out a .22. More of a girl's gun. But, not with that bad shoulder. Later on. It could be a little gift to celebrate you know what. Better than a ring. I seen nice .22s for about two hundred bucks. Have to keep it a secret though. Girls shouldn't have guns."

I smiled weakly over at him, nodding in anticipation of my substitute for a cheap gold band. His "girls shouldn't have guns" comment flew in the face of 200,000 American women in active military service—and thousands of frontier women who bagged game to keep their families fed.

The faintest bit of encouragement spurred Jerry on like a rutting boar as he clamped onto my good shoulder, splaying eager fingers that seemed to have tripled in length. Time to trim his tusks.

"I can't bear any pressure on this shoulder that Enoch broke so brutally," I forced two bulbous tears to pool in my eyes, though I wanted to laugh at my own cleverness in stopping an assault and dissing Jerry's competition in the same breath.

Jerry pulled back and composed his face into something that I suppose could suggest a mixture of plaintiveness and regret. "I might have been a bit forceful when I found you wandering like you was lost in that alley in Spokane. I was agitated, Jenny. Beside myself. It's a temper thing.

Can't be helped. Get it from my pa. You understand I'd never do nothing really bad to someone as pretty as you. Sometimes Enoch don't have half a brain."

Within the space of a few words, Jerry had foisted his behavior onto his father's genes, absolved himself from the guilt of choking me senseless due to agitation, assured me that if he hurt me it wouldn't be "bad," and computed the size of Enoch Bonner's brain.

Images of abused women with their battered faces and powerless eyes flashed before me. Compos mentis shot to hell from blows that broke more than bones.

It took all the strength I could muster to utter my next words to him. "Marybeth will be *agitated* if we don't get back to her prune cake. We've been gone almost two hours. If we're late, she'll report to Mr. Darken."

We chugged up from the side of the canyon, hit a gravel road, and hurtled along with rocks shooting in all directions as Western Yarrow, Arrowleaf Balsam Root, and Larkspur cowered alongside the road.

"I could wile away the hours, consulting with the flowers," I hummed softly, thinking of Dorothy's kindly scarecrow wishing that he had a brain. At that moment, I considered Ray Bolger to be the sexiest man Hollywood had ever produced.

CHAPTER 13

Twitching with the awkwardness of a boy on a first date, a man-sized Enoch Bonner stood on Mrs. Barnes's front porch the next afternoon as Marybeth whispered something that turned him the color of a boiled beet. Then, she blurted out: "If I was a bettin' woman, my money'd be on a boy like you, Enoch. Though I don't know why you'd be interested in someone as irksome as my stepdaughter." She tugged on his arm, wedging him into the parlor as though her knee had become a fulcrum.

She shot me a look of revulsion. "Nothin' but trouble since the three of them come here. Still, a man's hankerings ain't to be questioned." She patted his shoulder affectionately. "You done me a good turn when you tried to protect me."

Enoch colored again, the exact color of Mother's pink panties Marybeth had been wearing when I flattened her in front of the saints for twisting my little sister's arm.

With the handicap of half a brain, he had the good sense to shrug off Marybeth's hand and attempt an apology. "I just meant to move you away from that gun Jerry was waving around, Jenny. I never meant to knock you down . . . much less break your . . ."

"Shoulder. Dislocated. Not broken, Enoch. An accident. That's the way I think of it."

I smiled sweetly at Marybeth. "Is the clock running, Marybeth? We can drive around for *only* two hours?"

Enoch stared hopefully at Marybeth as he flopped his pickup keys from hand to hand nervously.

"If you happen to be a little bit late, I don't think nothing would come of it. It ain't Jenny I'd be worried about." She snorted and took off down the hall toward the kitchen, flinging two words behind her: "Pudding later."

"Marybeth must be fond of you, Enoch. She thinks her trademark puddings are Cordon Bleu concoctions."

"Whatever that means." Enoch swung the door wide and made a sort of bow. "Most of us avoid her food at pot-luck suppers. I hope she didn't ruin them quail I brung you."

I suddenly remembered that sad little wreath of birds that had been left by Enoch at Mr. Darken's door weeks ago. The tiny, buckshot-ridden bodies fried into brownish humps had been offered up as an "out-of-season treat" with gravy the consistency of wallpaper paste.

"What an unusual gift, Enoch. Something I would never dream of anyone giving me." *Not in my worst nightmare.* I patted his arm in a friendly fashion to counter the instinctive revulsion I was feeling for someone who would slaughter harmless little birds bobbing along through the underbrush.

"I thought a town girl like you probably never et such as them. I'm a good shot." Enoch's chest expanded exponentially as he flung open the driver's door of an older model pickup. The gleaming barrel of a gun was cradled behind the front seat.

"Heard you come across that grizzly and her cub yes-tiddy. I'm takin' precautions."

"I thought grizzlies were an endangered species," I said as gravely as if I were a founding member of the Sierra Club and stepped up onto an old-fashioned running board.

"Threatened," Enoch responded. "Pop 'em if they bother cattle. Pa skint one. Nice rug."

Remembering the expression in that grizzly mother's eyes as she turned away from Jerry holding me toward her like a tempting hors d'oeuvre, a brief wave of nausea swept over me. I'd take Enoch in another direction.

Someone with a head-sized bowl already had. Like Moe from the Three Stooges, his new haircut capped his head like a furry pelt. An inch-wide line of pale skin circled the space above his ears like a skunk's stripe. His madras plaid shirt had been starched so crisply that the fabric actually stood on its own away from his body. The scent of Old Spice warred with a tree-shaped deodorizer hanging from the mirror labeled "old leather."

Both Enoch and his old pickup were shipshape for our little outing. I needed to make an effort if I expected to get anything more than monosyllables out of Enoch this afternoon.

I patted the dashboard. "Antique pickup, Enoch? I love the running boards. Such style," I purred.

If I had learned one thing from that day on the Oregon Coast in Uncle Hal's boat, it was that setting the hook was the key to getting the fish.

"This here's a 1950 Chevy. Just got the rear bumper chromed again. Motor and tranny been replaced over the years, but she still runs good. Take you just about any place you want to go long as the road's decent."

"Could we drive along all the roads in the Compound, Enoch? I have such a bad sense of direction." *Another little lie.* "I found a little sketch of the original roads that Mr. Marchman laid out." I handed my drawing to Enoch. Actually, I made the sketch based on Marchman's notes about clearing tracks through the forest the width of 9.144 meters—30 feet to accommodate wagons—and added all the roads I could see in the distance.

"I can do better than that. I can show you the location of every original homestead. My folks go back a couple of generations. When he come, Pa's grandpa cleared all them old roads again. Some are still used, but some growed over now; Pa showed me exactly where they was."

I positively beamed at Enoch. His grammar left something to be desired, but his knowledge of Mr. Marchman's original compound would be priceless.

Without music or much conversation, for two hours, Enoch drove that rattling old truck sedately down graveled roads, along vague trails that led into the forest, aside the edges of furrowed fields, and around barns and sheds on what appeared to be private properties. Occasionally, someone in a field or coming out of a barn would glance our way and go on about their business.

Enoch grinned at my quizzical expression. "Pa's truck. No one questions where an elder goes. Pa don't have much use for fancy vehicles. He said it was a good thing that Mr. Darken sold that big Chrysler of his to someone on the Res. I guess you were pretty impressed with Jerry's new truck."

"Not in the least," I assured him. The way he drove it up and down those canyon walls terrified me." I scooted across the broad flat seat closer to Enoch. I was the one who had urged Jerry to drive into the canyon and up onto the mesa-like ridges beyond it. The lie tasted sugary in my mouth. I'd find something else to blame on Jerry—without actually naming him and do my damnable best to cultivate Enoch. He didn't seem so bad. I just wasn't interested in anything he had to say.

"We have time left to visit more, Enoch. Tell me about yourself. Where did you go to school?"

"Here."

"And your teachers?"

"Miz Darken grades one ... uh ... through four. . . I think."

Like a faulty ticker tape, Enoch's thought processes slogged along sporadically.

"She had us sing 'we're all in our places with sunshiny faces' until I wanted to puke."

The first genuine grin popped out just like Moe's when he's done a slapstick routine. I grinned back in encouragement.

"Then Miz Barnes took over for harder math like geometry and stuff we might need for carpentry work. Maylene Darken read us 'Hiawatha' and 'The Ride of Paul Revere' and called it history. Math with her was puzzling." Enoch sounded as though he still might be puzzled by math.

I thought about Maylene. She had probably tried to help me as best as she could with those subtle warnings about Mr. Darken's shady disposition.

A livelong prisoner falls into a routine that is hard

to break. She hadn't gone over to the dark side like Patty Hearst suffering from Stockholm Syndrome, but Maylene has no sense of logic. One thing does not lead to the next unless she can make it rhyme.

Just as Enoch turned his pickup alongside the large pond where Jerry had dumped my friend Abigail's body, I felt a sudden rush of anger.

I could number people that I trusted in this Compound on three fingers: Magdalene Marchman, Helen Barnes, and Josh Barnes. Mother and Lorena put their trust in me. It didn't go both ways. I couldn't rely on a mother who was still being shod by Manolo Blanik or a seven-year-old who would sell her birthright to keep her kitten. My mother and my sister were both simply children.

Just as I was reaching the boiling point, ruminating over the ills of this place like a cow with a cud, Enoch slammed on the brakes.

"I near forgot. Ma ast me to stop by Miz Grund's for a quart of honey. We'll take that short cut behind the barn and up the back way."

This was the same route Bonita and I had taken a couple of nights ago when I set up the little tête-à-tête between her and Josh. Josh had reluctantly agreed to go along with my plan so I could meet with Magdalene. He knew nothing about her will with both of our names on it—a secret between Magdalene and me.

Just as we came up the road by the barn, there he was—flaxen-haired Alexander on his splendid black horse Bucephalus. I might have gasped aloud at the glory of Josh astride that ebony, snorting horse.

Enoch glowered straight ahead as I hung my head out the window, looking back as he sped past, hoping Josh would see me watching him.

"Take a last look at both them two studs, Jenny." His tone was hateful.

"Miz Barnes's stallion will be going to the highest bidder soon. When Bonita's pa gets here from Boise tomorrow to take her home, Josh goes with them as far as Boise then on to another Compound."

"But his mother is . . ."

"Is scheduled for her Celestial Ceremony with Elder Grund on Sunday, two days from now. Jerry thinks it'll be a twofer. He's done ast for the Honeymoon Retreat to be reserved. Elder Grund don't need it."

Enoch hacked up something that might have been a laugh, then fell silent as he whipped the Chevy up a narrow winding road that led to the back of the Grund house. He slammed on the brakes so hard that his prized truck quivered in disbelief.

"Wait here in the pickup. I'll be back with the honey in a jif. Miz Grund's expectin' me. Not the crazy one," he snarled at me as though he knew I was in cahoots with Magdalene.

Ever since Enoch had said: "Jerry thinks it'll be a twofer," his face had resumed that odd beet-red color it had when Marybeth was whispering to him on the porch. I needed to think of something to convince him that Jerry would be sleeping solo in the Honeymoon Retreat.

From where I sat in the idling pickup, I could see row after row of Griselda's bee hives. In the distance, an old rock outcropping rose like jagged teeth, dozens of triangles atop a massive wall of rock. Jerry had driven his fancy Dodge truck along the backside of that ridge and said something about an old Indian burial ground on the other side.

I rolled down my window and almost swooned from the heavy scent of lavender, an entire field of purple just to the east of the hives. Enoch was nowhere in sight, so I slipped out of the pickup and skirted around the hives, heading toward the odd structure of rocks about sixty yards away.

Even from this distance, I could see that the rocks were honeycombed with small perforations that are called fretting or stone lattice. It was an odd geological formation so far from an ocean where salt water erodes rocks in this pattern.

Masses of blackberry fronds looped along the front of the rock, making a formidable barrier with their thorny branches. Griselda had mentioned that she moved the hives away from an old burial ground, but I could see nothing that looked the least bit like a cemetery. No stones. No tatty plastic flowers.

"Jenny! Get back here! You don't know what's in them woods." Enoch's basso stopped me short as I perused the area one more time. Being ordered about like a difficult child annoyed me to the extreme. Being told that Jerry had reserved the Honeymoon Retreat sent shivers down my very stiff spine.

Enoch sat in his truck with a pouting mouth that gave his bovine face the expression of a disgruntled cow with full udders. "I couldn't see where you went, Jenny. You just disappeared. Hold this for Ma." He handed me a quart jar of golden honey with a thick comb squashed against the sides of the glass.

Shoving the Chevy in gear, Enoch drove partway down the hill, pulled over to the shoulder, and turned off the ignition. "Jerry's been sayin' as how he saved you from that grizzly and you're bespoken for."

A most unladylike snort erupted from me followed by the only epithet that Enoch might appreciate: "Horse manure."

"Someone as pushy as Jerry assumes too much. I'm fifteen years old, Enoch. I've got places to go, things to see." My pleading tone hadn't lowered the hue of Enoch's flushed face. I had to try harder. I needed a driver, because I had considerable exploring left to do in the Compound; the prison walls seemed to be closing in.

"That being said, I prefer a laid-back kind of boy. Reasonable. Slow and steady." I could feel Enoch stretching his foot toward the brake pedal in an attempt to fit the bill.

"Jerry said that a classy girl like you wouldn't have nothin' to do with some old stick-in-the-mud like me. That's what he said. He said you'd never drive around with me if Mr. Darken didn't make you. He said I didn't have a chance." Enoch colored in a most unattractive way as a roseate flush settled around his thick neck.

I lifted my good arm and patted his hand. "I much prefer driving around with you, Enoch. Mr. Darken demanded that I spend an equal amount of time with both you and Jerry. That isn't my choice."

My choice would be to never speak to one of these cretins again, but without a choice, I needed to sharpen theirs gaffs and hope the roosters would go for each other while I looked for a way out of the Compound. "I really enjoy being with . . ."

It might have been the sound of the sea thundering in my ears as I rolled around like Deborah Kerr in the surf with Burt Lancaster. It wasn't. It was the sound of pent-up testosterone breaking through the floodgates.

Enoch's thick lips attached themselves to my open mouth like a remora—one of those suckerfish that can hardly be pried off its victim.

My dislocated shoulder screamed, because I could not possibly have produced a noise with that fat, groping tongue exploring my tonsils.

Then Enoch joined me in a scream as my right knee caught him dead center, mid-crotch. "Damn it all to hell, Jenny!"

Enoch cupped his hands over his crotch and laid his head across the steering wheel, whimpering in pain. "I only done what Marybeth said you liked. What all town girls like." His tears flowed down my legs like warm lava.

Or honey. "Your mother's honey didn't survive that burst of passion, Enoch." I scooped up a large hunk of honeycomb from amidst the glass shards and held it out toward him.

Dozens of waxy hexagonal fragments clung to my fingers. *Platonic solids as only nature could form them. Except for Enoch's snuffling, it would have been a magical moment.*

My instant flashback to Daniel Marchman's sketches of polyhedrons in his second journal made me want to shriek with that old Greek Archimedes: "Eureka, I've found it!" Those drawings were just the kind of ciphers I would have expected from a man who loved the geometry of surveying—and dropping clues.

I now knew the general location of where a cave and tunnel might be found—just to the south of where he'd staked out his claim 160 years ago. Fighting my way through flesh-ripping blackberry brambles to hunt for an entrance was another matter.

So was the sniveling hulk of a disappointed suitor in the front seat of an old pickup with me.

"Regardless of what Marybeth told you, Enoch, no girl—city or country mouse—wants to be attacked without so much as a warning."

"Mouse? I never said . . ."

A blank expression had settled on Enoch's face. It was more tolerable than the pained one. Did these people not even read *Aesop's Fables* to their children? No wonder they become barbarians.

"If you'll drive me home immediately, I'll forget this entire episode," I said self-righteously. My arm had worked its way out of the sling, and my shoulder felt almost normal. Hacking through blackberry bushes might be manageable.

The strained expression on Enoch's face as he shifted gears suggested that he might not forget an insult to his manhood so quickly.

CHAPTER 14

Enoch would never reveal that a mere girl had walloped his balls when he tried to canoodle her, but someone was not saying anything. The tension around the dinner table that evening with Mrs. Barnes and Bonita suggested that something was seriously amiss.

Bonita lifted her perfectly heart-shaped face as though posing for a Renaissance painter and sighed loudly. "It isn't fair, Mrs. Barnes. It isn't at all fair for Pa to take me when I just got here and was getting to be friendly with . . ." she paused and smiled slyly at me. "Jenny. We have so much in common."

Age. Gender. Lust for Mrs. Barnes's gorgeous son, Josh. That about did it for what we had in common.

"Maybe Marybeth can talk your father into letting you stay a little longer, Bonita. I've simply loved having both of you girls in the house with me. It's felt so empty since they moved Josh to SYM. I'm hoping they'll let him move back home."

If Bonita looked like the facsimile of a Renaissance painter's disappointed Madonna, Helen Barnes was Michelangelo's Mary. Her face was pale as ivory, her eyes so full of hopelessness that I wanted to cry for her.

Obviously, she didn't have clue about what the elders had been plotting to do with Josh. During our ride earlier in the afternoon, Enoch had let it slip that Bonita's father was taking Josh as far as Boise tomorrow to disappear into another compound farther away.

I watched Bonita shoving her mashed potatoes into a little rectangle with the right-hand side scooped out. She placed one green pea near the top and another about a third of the way down the left-hand side. "We're here." She popped the first pea into her mouth. "Now, I'll be there." She popped in the next pea and burst into tears.

A mashed potato map of Idaho. Distance and loss calculated by two boiled peas. Bonita never failed to amaze me. Maybe this weeping girl and I had more in common than I cared to admit.

The banging on the front door was loud enough to splinter it away from its hinges, but the door swung open under its own volition as Marybeth and Mr. Darken spoke in unison. "Your boy. Do you know where he is?"

Moving to the side of Josh's mother quickly, I held her protectively against me and shouted: "In that SYM prison where you keep boys against their will."

"Enough, Jenny." Mr. Darken's head bobbed sideways like one of those solar-powered toy monkeys. "The boys haven't seen him since early this afternoon when he went to work out the stallion."

"They didn't say nothin' until it got dark. They didn't want to cause trouble for Josh, but they got worried some-thin' mighta happened. That horse is temperamental. Down-right dangerous." Marybeth's eyes scanned Helen's face as though eager to see fear.

"But Josh? What could have . . . where is the horse? Is it all right? Josh sometimes leaves it in that far corral. Bucephalus doesn't like being stabled. Have you checked that pen?"

For a loving mother with a missing son, Mrs. Barnes seemed to be more interested in the welfare of a horse.

Bucephalus. I knew that horse would be named for Alexander's stallion. I also knew that at this moment, Josh was off to the battle of Issus—or, at the least, riding hell bent for leather through a fir forest on his way to the Res. Mrs. Barnes was stalling for time. I'd help her.

"Enoch and I saw him out behind the barn very late this afternoon when we were coming back from our ride. He was working the horse, putting him through his paces. I expect he's just riding him around in the pasture someplace." I added limply.

"You were home in the *middle* of the afternoon, not late, young lady. No one has seen Josh or the horse for the last four hours." Marybeth pointed outside to three pickups idling in the circular drive. "They checked all the roads. We suspect he's run off. Taken the stallion that by rights belongs to Elder Grund."

She glared over at Bonita and me. "We think somebody give him a heads up that he was bein' transferred down to the compound in the southeast part of the state tomorrow."

Bonita squealed like a scalded cat. "Not me, Marybeth. I didn't tell. I didn't even know."

The shudder that ran through Mrs. Barnes knotted me against her closer than my own shadow. She looked dead ahead at the two invaders. "Neither did I."

For once, Mr. Darken appeared faintly embarrassed. "We

thought it was for the best. For your boy and you, seeing as how he is opposed to you joining Elder Grund in wedlock."

"The opposition is mutual, Mr. Darken. I'd appreciate it if you and Marybeth left now. I'm quite sure your spy outside would have reported if Josh were here." She pointed to a shadow standing by the front porch.

Marybeth shoved past Mr. Darken and wiggled her fingers at Bonita. "Get your things together, Bonita. You're coming home with me. Your pa will be here early in the morning and expect you to be ready."

"But I want to . . . I'm worried about Josh. And Mrs. Barnes. She likes having me here. She said so." Bonita clamped onto Josh's mother with crab claw fingers.

"Do as Marybeth says, Bonita. Surely your father will let you visit again. No harm in that, is there?"

Not if the object of Bonita's affection had flown the coop so to speak. I patted Bonita's shoulder sympathetically and urged her up the stairs to help her pack. Things were heating up in the Compound. I needed to investigate that honey-combed rock face near Magdalene's house. Bonita would be a hindrance.

So would the cordon of CPRCers standing guard around the house. Just as they were leaving, I heard Mr. Darken mutter to the man on the porch: "Her son might come for her. They tried it once before. Until she's sealed, Elder Grund wants the property under surveillance."

Surveillance meant that shadows with Uzis paced the perimeter all night. Every time I crept out of bed to check on the possibility of a little excursion to that rock structure beyond Griselda's hives, a pervert was in sight.

AT THE BREAKFAST table, Josh's mother stared morosely with red-rimmed eyes into her granola. "He's safe, Jenny. He made it. Otherwise, the bell on the barn would have sounded to bring back the searchers.

"Why do they care so much? They were going to send Josh away. He's nothing to them."

"He isn't, but what he took with him is. My husband paid a considerable amount for the stallion. His bloodline goes back to Dash for Cash. Cyrus Grund wants that horse." She gave me a hopeful look. "Josh's name is on the papers. He has them."

She pushed back from the table abruptly. "Jenny, go into the office and pull down the shade. Do something to keep the watchers from being suspicious. Anything we do differently alerts them. I don't usually lower that shade until the afternoon sun hits it."

One of the watchers had to be a younger brother of Enoch Bonner. The bowl haircut and doltish expression marked him as kin. His face was as close to the window as he could get without fusing skin to glass. I strolled into the room casually without looking in his direction and pulled up my dress.

His gaze simmered with vulgarity—not desire. Something too dirty to name. That boy couldn't be more than thirteen. He was old enough to flush with the shame of being caught when I flipped him the bird and yanked down the old-fashioned, spring roller shade.

With a finger to her mouth, Mrs. Barnes tiptoed into the room. "Marybeth is coming up the walk. I need to check the desk. Stand against the door. She doesn't respect locks."

I flinched at the noise of the old tambour as she rolled

up the desktop. Marybeth's hearing was keen as an owl's. Her large ear holes were obvious, but somewhere above eye level must have been another pair.

Removing one of the small drawers, Mrs. Barnes groped around for a second and smiled reassuringly. "He took them. That night you met with Magdalene. He climbed up by the wisteria but went out through the office window. All the deeds and papers are gone."

"No dowry, huh?" I grinned back at her. "Cyrus might not be such an eager bridegroom."

We could hear the front door slamming behind Marybeth. "Oh, he's eager. Legal documents don't mean much to the elders. Cyrus thinks he can take everything if the Council approves. And they have."

The color drained from her face so abruptly that I automatically checked the floor by her feet for blood as the door shook from a vigorous whack.

"You need to get out here, Helen, and quit whisperin' behind closed doors. I've come to help you sort what needs to be moved to the Grund house. Cyrus says you'll go on home with him Sunday after the Sealing. Elder Bonner's boys will bring a truck for personal things you want moved. So's the Wilson family can move in."

She shoved open the door and looked suspiciously at both of us. "Jenny, you'll be coming home Sunday morning. Your ma will be right happy to see you." Marybeth beamed with the expression of someone who had just delivered a death warrant wrapped up in red ribbon.

"Why don't you whip up some of that good egg salad, Marybeth? I need Jenny to help me decide what to take. I've been too worried about Josh to think about the ceremony."

The word "ceremony" rose and fell as Mrs. Barnes stood at attention, her left arm limp, and her right hand lifting an invisible bugle to play taps. Then, her hand tucked itself into my arm; we marched away up the stairs. For once, Marybeth didn't follow.

Shades of that minty celadon green of Chinese porcelain on the walls of bedroom walls of Mrs. Barnes's bedroom conjured up a calmness that neither of us was feeling. "Quickly, Jenny. Move boxes; yank clothes off the hangers. Make noise. We need to talk before Marybeth gets up here. She can hear through walls."

I dragged an old camelback trunk across the floor, making as much noise as possible, and whispered: "Josh is probably at the Earnshaw's house by now. That's where he took me when he found me sick and lost in the forest."

"I'm not worried about Josh. I know he's safe with Izzy Earnshaw. I'm worried about *you*, Jenny. Marybeth is taking you home Sunday for a reason. I'm afraid that reason is Jerry Winner. I heard a couple of the men outside make a lewd comment yesterday about a double Sealing Ceremony."

"I'd put Cleopatra's asp to my throat, jump in the river faster than Ophelia, pour poison down my throat like Juliet rather than . . ." Suicidal images of literary heroines were coming fast and thick. It must have been the mention of Aunt Izzy who loved to bring literature to life.

"It's not the time for levity, Jenny. Things are afoot here that are out of our control." She clutched my hand.

This frightened woman did not need to know my hair-brained idea about where I thought I might find a tunnel. She needed legal advice. "This is the United States of America. Women cannot be forced into marriage against their will. And, it is illegal for someone to marry a fifteen-year-old. I've got almost a year to escape." I spoke with more confidence than I was feeling.

"Maylene was fourteen when she married Gomer. Marybeth was fifteen. I don't think you'll get much sympathy from that quarter." Her shoulders drooped. "I was considered a spinster because I didn't marry until I was twenty-two."

"But of your own free will?"

"Of course. My husband and I don't believe in polygamy—or many of the things that are going on here." She looked expectantly toward the stairs, as though the footsteps resounding on them might be her husband's.

I quickly folded a stack of dresses I'd pulled off hangers, whipped a sling back around my arm that no longer needed support, and tried to look as busy as a one-armed paper hanger when Marybeth cracked open the door.

"Jenny, I need you to peel them eggs. You can do that one-handed. Come on downstairs. Let Helen have some peace before her special day."

As I followed Marybeth down the stairs, I could see her heaving shoulders. She might have been weeping for Helen Barnes, but I doubted it.

CHAPTER 15

For a bright Saturday Idaho day, gloom hung about in the house like the odor of mold—musty with volatile organic compounds brewing in spite of Marybeth's cleaning.

Josh's mother spent most of the day listlessly tossing photograph albums and letters into boxes as I taped and stacked them.

"What I care about is on those photos and in the letters—good memories with family and friends. The Wilsons are welcome to this house. Without my husband and Josh, it has ceased to have any meaning for me."

The finality in Mrs. Barnes's voice reminded me of that terrible rainy day in Portland when I stared at vile synthetic grass trying its dead level best to hide my father's grave.

She needed cheering up. "I might have discovered something. I'm not sure, but I have an idea about the tunnel."

"That's a myth, Jenny. There is no tunnel. The early settlers probably found some kind of cave to hide in and store food when roving bands of Shoshone or Nez Perce came to the Compound. The local Skitswish were friendly. Those are Izzy's people." Her pellucid blue eyes were tearing.

"I pray that Josh is with them now—just as you should be."

A burst of "in the sweet by and by we shall meet on that beautiful shore" sailed past us just a step off key.

"Marybeth is in a rare mood today. Beware of her, Jenny. She has it in for you. She asked me if I could find my old wedding veil. I don't think she was suggesting I wear it at the Sealing tomorrow." She pointed toward the rusting 50-gallon trash drum in the back yard. "It's going up in smoke."

Also going up in smoke were any plans I had to explore that rock cliff near Magdalene's house. My excuse to leave the house was flattened as resoundingly as Marybeth's pancakes.

"I'll go ask Griselda for another jar of honey for Mrs. Bonner. I accidentally broke the one Enoch got for her yesterday."

"The Bonners is off limits to you, Jenny. Gomer has drummed Enoch out of the Corps so to speak. Them boys got into fisticuffs last evening. No more ridin' around." Marybeth whirled on me and tucked in that pendulous bottom lip, as though she had said too much.

In a wheedling tone, she continued. "The original pact seems the best solution. Elder Winner and Gomer are meeting tonight. I don't need to hear none of your fancy arguments. It's done. Your ma might have a nice dress you could borry."

"No chador? No burqa?" I asked icily, refusing to be llamannihilated by Marybeth. "If you think that I'll go quietly into purdah, you've got another . . ."

"Speak civil English, Jenny. Not them foreign words,"

she interrupted. "I got somethin' your ma give me for you. You ain't deserving, but I promised. Maybe, it'll calm you down."

The cloying humility on her cadaverous face would have bested Uriah Heep as she handed me a small, sealed envelope with "Jenny" scrawled in pencil on the front in my mother's handwriting.

Taking two steps at a time, I dashed up the stairs to my bedroom and ripped open the envelope. Inside was a coarse sheet of lined paper torn from a Big Chief tablet.

My mother's notes on the frig at home were always terse: *don't forget milk; get socks for Lorena; dress warm; rent late—avoid mgr.*

This one was in sync with her style but vague as to purpose: *Meet me after dark at Retreat. Don't tell. Secret.*

For the first time after my second kidnapping—the one in which Mother wasn't complicit—I felt an uncomplicated rush of affection for her.

Mother was frightened of the dark, yet she had planned a clandestine meeting at the Retreat. That place gave both of us the willies. She must have an important secret to share.

The last secret Mother had shared with me was the bombshell she dropped at my father's gravesite: "Your father's brother should have been here." First I'd ever heard about an uncle. She didn't bother to add that he was an identical twin.

My Uncle Hal might have been a facsimile of my father, but in their case, blood wasn't thicker than water. At this moment, Uncle Hal was probably bobbing along the Oregon Coast in his fishing boat without a second thought for his desperate niece.

If I were going to elude those two guards posted at the house tonight to meet Mother at the Retreat, I needed to do considerable thinking and planning.

I reviewed famous prison escapes in my mind. In the Seventeenth Century, Grotius crawled into a chest drilled full of air holes and left his wife behind in prison to explain. Dillinger put shoe polish on a fake gun and spooked the guards. Some Alcatraz escapees left plaster dummies of their heads in their beds.

The voice of another dummy yelled up the stairs: "Jenny, I'm going on home now. Helen went to bed with a headache. I give her somethin' to help her sleep. I fried up half a chicken in case she gets hungry. All the excitement of the relocation musta got to her. I'll be here early in the mornin'."

Just as Marybeth stepped off the porch, she shouted back at me. "Don't forget to feed them hens and lock up the coop before dark." She stuck her head back inside the door. "I forget and left them chicken entrails in that pail just inside the kitchen door. Dump 'em in the barrel."

Whether she realized it or not, Marybeth had provided an escape route. A trip to the hen house or setting a fire in the trash barrel at sunset might create just the escape diversion I needed.

"Be very careful, Jenny. They're watching both of us. I've lowered all the shades, but I saw two men and a boy on guard. I put together a survival kit in a backpack for you in the office if you get a chance." Mrs. Barnes eased up behind me.

The chance might be on Mother's note in my pocket. I didn't want to raise any false hopes, but I'd made it through the broken section of the electric fence in the canyon once; I could do it again.

As though she were reading my mind, Mrs. Barnes said: "The men fixed that part of the fence where you got through once. They have this placed locked down. I don't know how Josh got out."

I did. I saw him jump Bucephalous like a Lipizzaner over a stack of firewood. That stile in the blackberry thicket where the women cross over to pick berries outside the Compound would be smooth sailing.

"I'll help you in any way that I can, Jenny, but Cyrus has me on lockdown in my own house—you too, but you are faster." A sad, single tear dripped down her face. "Being too emotional won't help. It never does. I'll go fix us some chamomile tea. Peter Rabbit's mother thought it helped."

SHE WAS RIGHT about me being faster. Instead of feeling like the swift-footed Achilles, I felt like the soothsayer Calchas as I looked over at the chicken entrails putrefying in a zinc bucket by the door; I knew all things past and all things to come. At the moment, the world looked very grim.

Sherlock would examine everything with skepticism; he would be inclusive, not miss a thing. I pulled out Mother's note and sniffed it. Not a whiff of the White Linen Mother wore. Just a faint odor of lye soap, Rueful Rosemary, Marybeth's favorite. She had handed me the note. Sion Soap eclipses all. I should do their marketing.

The hands on Mrs. Barnes's Waterbury clock bisected the face of the clock precisely. At least two hours before I'd dare venture out. Maybe Mother had found a way for us to leave. That might be her secret. In the meantime, I'd gnaw my way through Marybeth's greasy chicken while I waited for the sun to descend. I might need protein for the night ahead.

I FOUND EXACTLY what I needed in that little closed-in porch off the kitchen—32 ounces of Coleman Kerosene in a handy bottle. The opening gambit would be a trip to close the henhouse—just as Marybeth had told me to do. *I never do anything right according to her.*

If I dumped the pail of entrails with a half-full bottle of fuel into the trash barrel on my way back, the sides of that rusty barrel might just explode.

I wasn't exactly in the league of Moriarty. Sherlock called that fiend the Napoleon of crime. But, I was feeling a bit full of myself.

I'd flash a lot of leg on the way to the henhouse to be sure the guards were watching me. I needed to balance the sack of corn atop the pail of chicken guts that concealed the kerosene.

With my sling back in business, I'd be just a clumsy, one-armed city girl—struggling with a sack and a pail and a henhouse door. If the guards found a helpless female amusing, they'd really get a kick out of one carelessly drizzling kerosene inside a straw-filled henhouse, a girl who then would manage to dump a half-full bottle of fuel along with chicken entrails into a barrel of smoldering trash.

WHEN THE BIG kaboom skyrocketed viscera and what might have been a few fragments of a wedding veil heavenward, several chickens may have been roasted at just after 8 p.m.

From the squawking and shouting I could hear as I rounded the house, the Wilsons would be in need of a new henhouse. A crescent moon hung like a golden amulet just over the tips of fir trees in the distance.

I could see the tacky chalet, the Honeymoon Retreat, like a pustule on the side of a hill about a quarter of a mile ahead of me. Mother would be waiting on that rickety front porch to reveal her secret. She might have Lorena with her. We would leave. I could get them through that electric fence by disconnecting one of the battery-powered fence controllers down the line.

I paused for a moment, heaving with exertion and stress. I hadn't brought the survival kit Mrs. Barnes put together. Mother and Lorena might need it if we trekked into the forest.

Glancing back at a blaze lighting the dark night, I thought about Josh's mother. I hadn't brought her either. Josh would expect me to save his mother if I saved mine.

Not a light flickered in a window of the chalet. A canopy of stars hung so low in the black sky that the retreat popped out like a garish pink cube on a velvet painting.

No one was in sight. Mother must be up on the porch, waiting in the shadows, hiding. Marybeth had said that Mr. Darken was meeting with Elder Winner tonight. If Mother had avoided the sisterwives, she might have come earlier and gone inside.

Step at a time, I eased my way up half-rotten wood stairs that groaned in the silent night. The faintest whisper of something on the far edge of the porch stopped me. Nothing moved. Only the soft soughing of firs. I could hear my own breathing and an owl somewhere in the distance. It was too quiet. I shuddered involuntarily, thinking of Mother inside, alone, perhaps frightened too.

I dared not turn on my flashlight. Lights were bobbing across fields in the distance. The toll of a bell stopped me in my tracks. A couple of centuries ago, it would signal death—three for a man, six for a woman. But not after sunset. They'd wait, respectfully, for the sun to rise so that grief would not be intensified by the dark.

The resonant gong of this bell splintered the night, put me on edge, left me off guard. That's when I heard it.

Hitler's hobnailed jackboots make a distinctive sound, like rock being crushed with each step. Or the delicate vertebrae just between C2 and C3 crunching between calloused ham hands.

CHAPTER 16

I awoke in a pool of ripe, red blood so slick that I might have slid across it had it not been for the chalky white cords holding me spread-eagled in my own gore.

The steady drumming of Toby Keith screaming for "a little less talk and a lot more action" pounded in my head to let me know that I hadn't ascended to a heavenly concert.

Through a narrow slit in one of my eyes, I could see an almost naked Jerry in a rocking chair. His pale, concave chest resembled dough, but his boxer shorts sported green Mutant Ninja turtles with the word "awesome" dangling off to the side.

I squeezed my eye shut and tried to ignore Toby wailing about getting down to the main attraction. The attentive expression on Jerry's face suggested that necrophilia was not his bag. He was waiting for a live attraction.

Easing my ankles and wrists tentatively against those inflexible white ropes, I knew that I was in a tight spot. Damn that Marybeth. She didn't favor Enoch as a suitor for me. That was a ploy to hide her plotting with Jerry. That note from Mother was a forgery. Like a crafty criminal, Marybeth had the means, motive, and opportunity.

Triple whammy. Like Sherlock, I was just about to disappear at the hands of Moriarty—not even a monster with a keen mind that I could admire.

I thought about all those hours spent lying in my bed, weak in the knees, nipples on alert with a delicious longing for something magical to happen with Josh or Heath. Now, I longed to be one of those ancient asexual rotifers that reproduced without sex for millions of years.

Not on red polyester in the same bed where Mr. Darken had his way with Mother. If Jerry ravished me in this space at this moment in time, it wouldn't be just a membrane that was broken. It would be me. Jenny Hatchet. Who I am. It was about what I wanted and who I would never want.

I remembered looking at the photograph of that other Jenny Hatchet in Uncle Hal's house, the grandmother I had never seen and thinking about moments of space—not of time. We can't stop time, fast forward or reverse it. But moments in space can stay in our heads with memories of our own choosing. No one should be allowed to intrude on that space.

Jerry could fling me out the window like Jezebel for the dogs to eat, but I'd take on a ravaging army one by one before I'd let Jerry have his way with me.

I flexed my legs, feeling muscles digging into the slick polyester. Katy bar the door. A clever girl can win over brute force any day in the week.

I heaved my body, breasts first in Jerry's direction, blinked at the harsh light and in my best Mae West voice said: "How do you expect me to give you any pleasure with my hands and feet tied?"

Toby had returned to his theme of a "little less talk" that lit up Jerry's dull eyes like neon lights. "Cagey, ain't you, Jenny? A quick-broke mare is steady. The Sealing will be tomorrow. No one minds if the package is tampered with."

I shifted my bottom against the polyester bedspread. Aunt Izzy's lacy panties were intact.

Jerry stood. He moved toward the head of the bed on knobby knees like one of those long-billed wading birds unsure of the shore.

I needed to convince him that I was a femme fatale, not a fifteen-year-old virgin, frightened of what looked like a horseradish root pushing ahead in advance of Jerry. I tried to remember every word associated with sex.

"Fellatio can be nice. Or just simple bonking. Coition. You people probably call it making Whoopie." I peered up at him with what I thought was a seductive leer.

Even though I expected the blow, it caught me by surprise. I tasted a thin trickle of blood just at the corner of my mouth. I didn't flinch. I just called on Mae West to help me in my hour of need.

"Too much of a good thing can be wonderful, Jerry. Surely, someone who's been around like you would know that," I said seductively. I stared at his hairless chest. "Pounding on someone who can't move is like kneading dough. Boring. I'm a girl who likes foreplay."

"Our women don't talk nasty. We don't allow it. You better learn to shut that trap of yours when I say so, Jenny. Things will go easier when you don't cross me." Jerry unknotted one of the wrist ropes and moved down to my left ankle.

"The door is locked. My gun is in the corner. You can yell your head off, but no one will hear you. Even if they did, they wouldn't come. We don't hold with interference."

So none of the CPRCers interfered with the interferers up in the honeymoon house. Even if I got off a scream to wake the dead, no one would respond.

"Your ma and sister will be at the Sealing tomorrow. They'd be happier if you didn't look all beat up. It's a big occasion for both of us. We are supposed to be happy."

A glazed expression was settling behind Jerry's eyes as he watched me torque my body onto my left side and struggle to free my other hand.

He pulled a half-empty, three-liter bottle of red wine out of a brown paper sack. "Mogen David. Good stuff. The bride and groom can have it this one time. I done drunk quite bit waiting for you. I suspect you had something to do with that fire behind Miz Barnes's house. You wanna start another one?" He bleated like a strangled goat at his own cleverness.

The rope on my foot dropped away; I stretched my body full-length on the faux fibers, a fake sensuous movement—like a cat flexing to spring.

The two-foot long, old-fashioned boom box gyrated with yet another Toby Keith number. "Do you mind if I find something a bit more romantic, more soothing, Jerry?"

With one fluid movement, I rolled off the bed and stepped toward the boom box. Unsettled, Jerry turned and leaned over to set down the wine bottle.

At that moment, I experienced a rush of adrenaline as fierce as Samson must have felt when the re-grown locks of hair tickled his neck.

The boom box swung like a pendulum into the side of Jerry's skull. I might have been on one end of it, but the damage was too shocking to give that possibility a second thought. Fake red polyester is not the color of fresh blood. It pales in comparison.

CHAPTER 17

A s though the canopy of stars in the dark sky had dropped into the Compound, dozens of lights bobbed around the grounds in the distance. I could hear people shouting and an occasional engine starting with headlights flashing on the side roads.

The chalet behind me was quiet as a tomb. *I had just killed Jerry Winner and hadn't mopped up after myself. The crime scene was so full of my DNA that I'd be locked away for the rest of my life. No time to worry about that now. Any prison would be an improvement over the Compound.*

The wave of lights in the distance spread across the pasture that led to the canyon where Josh and I once had a picnic—and where I'd crawled under the electrified fence to freedom on the Res.

Only one guard appeared to be left at the Barnes's house. He slumped in the front porch swing with his chin resting against his chest and his gun on the floor.

Careful not to disturb him, I circled around to the back window. A wide swath had been ploughed around the smoldering ruin of a henhouse. The office window was wide open.

Stealthily, I approached it, but without Bonita to boost me up, I could only get the tips of my fingers across the high ledge.

The strong hands of a potter gripped mine and pulled me steadily up. "Thank God, Jenny. I had no idea what had happened to you. When the men could get close enough, they combed the burning timbers, searching for your body. That's when the alarm sounded. They knew you were running. Where were you?"

"In the Honeymoon Retreat trying to avoid a rapist," I said dourly. Badmouthing Jerry couldn't erase the image of those pale, chicken legs lolling out of those silly boxer shorts—as though they'd never take another walk in boots.

"I think I killed Jerry. He tied me to the bed. He'd been drinking. I talked him into untying me and smashed his head with a boom box." The words came out in a perfunctory fashion, as though I'd been interrogated so long that I had nothing more to hide.

"Oh, Jenny. I would never dream that Jerry would violate a young girl. I taught him in Sunday school. He's impulsive but . . .?"

"I think he missed hearing the beatitude about the meek inheriting the earth. He choked me, tied me up like an S and M expert, and was wearing only a goofy pair of boxer shorts when I conked him."

Fighting back tears, I added, "It wasn't just for me; I kept thinking about Abigail. How he just snapped her neck and threw her like a piece of garbage in that pond."

The arms that gripped me were lovingly firm and the voice so full of regret that I almost forgot to be afraid. "We should have known. Maylene suspected. That's why she put that high-necked robe on Abigail's body. We avoid questions so we won't be complicit."

Smiling, she said, "You had to protect your virtue," and touched my cheek. "Jerry will probably be OK. Superficial head wounds bleed profusely."

"Splattered. That's what his did." The memory of Jerry's head gushing like a fire hydrant wasn't as disturbing as those chicken-thin shanks of his lying so listlessly. I knew now why he favored knee-high boots.

My salacious report about Jerry's attempted rape seemed to disturb her more than what I did to his head with the boom box.

Even in the darkness of the room, I knew that something was different. Helen Barnes was wearing long pants and a black wool jacket. Her hair was tucked into a dark stocking cap. Soot smudged her face. She pointed to a pile of clothes in the corner. "Change, Jenny. Some of Josh's clothes. You can belt up the pants and roll the cuffs. That's his goose down jacket."

She glanced out the window. "They have a pattern they use for cordoning off this place. All the exits are blocked—east, west, and south. North is too mountainous. Josh and I made it as far as the highway once, because we weren't suspects."

She pointed toward the front porch. "I put the sleeping pills Marybeth left me in his milky drink. That's Enoch's brother. He'll just have a nice rest."

Mrs. Barnes leaned as far as possible out the window, looking left and right, while I yanked on Josh's clothes. I dug into the pocket of my dress for the piece of cloth with little metal loops that Magdalene had wrapped around her great-grandfather's journals.

Fearing to turn on a flashlight, I fingered my way along the shelves until I came to the journals. I had crammed Magdalene's will and property deeds into the back of the first journal. The sketch of the tunnel was on the last page of the second journal. I ripped it out, patted the fine leather cover as an apology, and tied the papers into a small bundle with the cloth Magdalene had used to wrap the journal. I stuck the seer stone in my pocket. Who knows what that might find?

Grabbing the survival kit, I gave a grim order: "Drop and run as fast as you can straight north, the back way to Magdalene's house, Mrs. Barnes. I'll be bringing up the rear."

"From now on, it's Helen. We're partners. And I'll bring up the rear. You're faster. You set the pace. You'll have a better chance if I don't slow you down."

If Helen Barnes had any qualms about heading toward the house where her groom-to-be might be struggling to keep his heart in working order until a Celestial Marriage the next day, she didn't say.

For an untrained runner, tearing off in the dead of night through rough terrain without the aid of a flashlight, Helen Barnes kept up a reasonable pace until we reached the fork in the path. She stumbled over to the fallen log where her son once sat with Bonita, and wheezed with exertion.

"You go on, Jenny. I need to rest a moment." Her voice sounded raspy.

"I need to rest too." The little lie offered me a moment to get my bearings. Covering the lens of my flashlight with my fingers, I allowed only a sliver of light to reveal lumpy tree roots in the narrow road leading up to Magdalene's house.

The phantasmagorical house jutted ahead of us like Dr. Frankenstein's hilltop castle. Behind us, I could hear a truck laboring up the hill, headlights flashing into the surrounding fir forest.

"That's the Bonner's truck. We need to get to the far side of the beehives and into those blackberry thickets as quickly as possible. Grab the back of my jacket and stay close," I urged Helen.

Pushing the backpack in front of me, I plunged into a thick cover of brush and razor-sharp blackberry vines. The ropy stalks sliced into us wickedly. Even the leaves were thorny. I remembered the myth about Bellerophon riding the winged stallion Pegasus to Mt. Olympus and falling into blackberry brambles. Maimed and blinded, he lived as an outcast.

I grasped Helen's hand. Being blind outcasts together was a better fate than ending up in the hereafter with the ghosts of Jerry Winner and Elder Grund as celestial companions. "Quick! Let's get over to that wall of rocks. Maybe we can hide from the lights of the truck."

Hundreds of small orifices in the rocks created a textured surface that would bloody the hands of anyone trying to climb them. Not daring to turn on my flashlight, I kept a firm lock on Helen's arm and steered her toward the far end of a rocky protrusion we could barely make out under the starry sky.

We could hear voices shouting as another truck pulled in behind the house. Lights came on as an upper window flew up with a bang. "The Sabine women escape you Roman heathens?"

It was Magdalene's voice, so gleeful that I felt infused with a burst of confidence. Almost 3,000 years ago, the Roman men had raided their Sabine neighbors for wives. I had the sense that Magdalene knew we were near and was creating a distraction.

Groping along the rocky structure like a mole with an extra polydactyl thumb because my eyes had become useless, I stopped and sniffed. A distinct current of air with a hint of ammonia came from where we stood next to that honeycombed ridge of rock.

The opening was about two feet—just the width for a bear to squeeze through for a nice, long hibernation. Or a cougar's den. They like mountain crevasses to hide their young. Or rabid bats.

Strobe lights pierced the blackberry brambles. We had no choice. "In here. We'll wait. Just crouch down near the opening in case we need to leave in a hurry." I could almost see the gleaming fangs of an irritated lodger.

From the backside of the house, we could hear Griselda arguing with Elder Bonner. "I don't care what you think, I saw two figures and a flash of light heading way off into the forest on the other side of the road."

"You're probably right. Nothing bigger than a fox could get through brambles this thick, Griselda. If they were here, they've taken the other path back towards the main gate. There's no getting out of this place tonight. Just lots of hidey-holes. I say we wait until morning when they'll surface," Elder Bonner sounded like a man who would rather set a trap than exert himself to follow his prey.

I felt Helen's arm tighten around me as we settled into what might have been just a scooped out place in the rock face or a cavern as big as Mammoth Cave with 300 miles of passageways.

WHEN THE TRUCKS pulled away and the house lights went out, we went into action. I aimed my flashlight at a ceiling that extended over our heads at least twenty feet and swooped the beam around us.

Maybe we'd be as lucky as Darwin in Wales when he found only an ancient rhinoceros's bones in a cave; or, we might be unlucky enough to disturb a grizzly's sleep.

Small piles of bones littered one area of the cave. Two twisting passageways branched in opposite directions. The air felt damp and cool.

"I can remember from the sketch of a tunnel in that old journal that we should go left at the first fork in the tunnel. We need to move away from the entrance. I don't trust those men not to return."

Stalagmites and stalactites paired in eerie splendor along the sides of a fairly flat gravel pathway into the cave. We'd walked for what seemed like more than an hour when a cavern opened ahead of us with a huge domed ceiling above and flat rocks beneath settled end-to-end, as tidy as a slate floor.

"Let's rest here for a minute, Jenny. We haven't slept

for hours. I raided Josh's camping supplies for the backpack. He and Heath did a lot of camping as boys." Helen rummaged around in the pack and pulled out a mini LED lantern and clicked it on.

The cave lit up like Christmas; the sheen of crystalline precipitates of calcite hung about us like the precious ornaments Mother would unwrap one at a time for Lorena and me to hang on our tree, as her own mother had done for her.

I didn't want Helen to see me getting emotional, so I did my own rummaging in the backpack. I needed to study the map. If we heard voices behind us, we should be ready to run in the right direction.

The piece of cloth that Magdalene had wrapped around her great-grandfather's journals fell out with a tiny clinking sound on the rock floor near the lantern.

Dazzling green lights flashed in dozens of directions. Garish costume jewelry rings had been sewn along the edges of the soft cloth.

Helen gasped and picked up the cloth. "This is Magdalene's blue cashmere scarf. And her rings." She fondled the rings. Blue stones, green stones, red stones and rhinestones.

"These are worth a fortune, Jenny."

"Stones that big can't be real. They make synthetic ones now that look so real you can't tell the difference," I said dismissively.

"Not for Magdalene," Helen retorted. "Her father bought her a new ring for every birthday. He was a very successful rancher. I was just a small child then, but I sat in the pew behind the Marchmans just so I could stare at Magdalene's beautiful hands—perfection of flesh and bone—the rings just amplified their beauty. I wonder why she gave them to you."

I mutely shook my head. She had made out her will to Josh and me. Who knows what Magdalene was thinking?

"I can guess." Helen was reading my mind again. "She quit wearing her rings after her father died. She and Cyrus had been married for only a year when he took Griselda as his second wife. That's when Cyrus sold all of Magdalene's horses. Left her at the mercy of himself or Griselda to drive her if she wanted to go to church."

The tears in Helen's eyes matched mine. "Cyrus is a dreadful man. She probably hid the rings to keep him from selling them. He humiliated Magdalene. Her life with him has been a misery."

"Let's take her with us!" My enthusiasm startled Helen. "I can double back, figure out how to get into her house, and bring her into the cave. I know I can!"

"I'm sure you can, but she can't."

"Can't what?"

"Leave. Walk that far. Not having a corrective procedure on her foot early on has caused other problems. She can walk only a limited distance. Besides, she'd never leave this place."

Helen stroked my hair as she talked. It comforted me. "Magdalene loves this land her great-grandfather claimed and the house he built. She'd be content if she could rid herself of Cyrus and Griselda—and fill her empty stable with horses again."

"But I thought Cyrus wanted Bucephalus, Josh's stallion."

"He does. For breeding. Magdalene's horses were like

her children. He broke her heart when he sold them. And that's the man the elders were going to saddle me with!"

My sharp intake of breath was the only noise before a burst of crystal-clear laughter sounded next to me.

"A joke, Jenny. Saddle. I was trying to lighten up things. We need to keep our spirits up if we're ever to find our way out of this cave." She patted the rock next to her. "Let's sit close—it's warmer that way—and study the map."

She pulled a brown paper bag out of the backpack. "Marybeth's chicken looked greasy, so I brought peanut butter sandwiches."

"That's a relief. I never want to think about Marybeth again. She tricked me into going to the Retreat with a note that was supposedly from Mother. I don't know why she hates me so much." I could think of dozens of reasons, but I didn't want Josh's mother to think ill of me.

"I blame Gomer Darken, not Marybeth, for the way she behaves. I've known her all her life. She was younger than my husband and me—a good-hearted girl." In the light reflected off the gleaming cave walls, Helen looked almost girlish. Marybeth looked like an old harridan.

"Younger than you?" I asked incredulously.

"Three years younger with a hopeless crush on my fiancé. When we went to the University, I was seventeen; Josh's father was nineteen. The Darkens had just moved to the Compound from somewhere back East. Brought in new money." Her tone suggested that the neighborhood had gone downhill when the Darkens arrived.

"Gomer's father had three wives and no other children. Gomer had been married to Maylene for several years before they moved. They seemed happy, but within a month, Gomer's father struck a deal with Marybeth's father. I told you that she was only fifteen. Her father gave her no choice."

She handed me a sandwich neatly wrapped in wax paper. "People with no choices have to try anything to remain sane."

I wondered if she was talking about herself or Marybeth.

"I just make more pots." Helen laughed, second-guessing me again.

"Marybeth, on the other hand, likes to *stir* the pot. Gomer dealt her a low blow when he surprised her by bringing home a new family. Your mother is a beauty. Poor Marybeth has been just this side of maniacal ever since she arrived. You have to try to understand her perspective."

In the darkness, I couldn't see Helen's face clearly, but I knew she was feeling sympathy for Marybeth. If that woman crawled on bloody knees screaming *mea culpa* from here to Becket's tomb, I'd never forgive her for whipping Lorena.

Marybeth's perspective defies logic. She leaps to a conclusion and conjures up facts to support it. For instance, cats belong outside; therefore, she was justified in switching Lorena's legs to reinforce that a natural law had been broken—along with the skin of a seven-year-old.

CHAPTER 18

Sitting on the hard damp rocks under points of stalactites that could pierce even Enoch's thick skull, I began to tick off the seven cardinal sins and match them to denizens of the Compound—a word association game to wile away time in this dark labyrinth without letting darker thoughts intrude, such as the possibility of dead batteries and the uncertainty where we were in this cave.

Word games were my antidote to stress. Sin was a fixation for the CPRC transgressors, so the word association was fitting. Wrath and Envy were well acquainted with Marybeth; Jerry cornered the market on Lust; Greed went hand in hand with all the elders. I had just begun to determine the best candidate for Gluttony when Helen interrupted my thought process.

"Peanut butter is so filling. I'm suddenly tired. Just a short nap would help. These stones are so cold and damp. I wonder if . . ." She aimed the beam of her flashlight over to the right wall of the cave and gasped.

Standing side by side like soldiers at arms, crates and boxes lined the far wall of the cave. Helen pointed her flashlight at one with big black letters spelling out "Harrison."

"That's my family name. My grandfather told me that his great-grandfather helped store supplies in a cave but was forbidden to speak of it."

Moving as fast as a whippet, she snatched a knife out of the backpack and began prying up boards on the top of the crate.

She tossed an odd striped thing toward me. "A Hudson Bay blanket—must be over one hundred years old but still intact. We can sleep on top of it." She scooped up some long, brown cylinders. "Beeswax candles. We might have a use for these."

Like a woman possessed, she pulled out cooking pots, saws, hammers, knives, and a large rotting burlap bag.

"This might have held dried beans or corn, but I think they sprouted in spite of the darkness. Lots of jars and a few cans at the bottom. And this." She held up a small leather pouch and brought it over to the lantern.

The stiff leather thong binding the top edge had adhered to the leather; when Helen rammed her knife into the bag, ten Liberty head twenty dollar gold pieces fell into a gleaming pile.

"You have the Midas touch, Helen. That's a good omen."

Better than that, I thought. Given the price of gold today and the possible historic value of those coins, Mrs. Barnes would walk out of the cave richer than she walked into it. If we ever found our way out.

I grabbed a small hand axe off the floor, checked the handle to be sure it was solid, and went to work on the next crate.

"Stop, Jenny! Those aren't ours. We can't . . ."

"Yes, we can. We might need what's inside. If you recognize any names of families still in the Compound, we can take anything valuable and return it some day. Not to the Winners or Bonners. They owe me." I whacked ruthlessly at the tops of the remaining crates while Helen sifted through their contents.

We netted several cans of rancid lard, dozens of soggy wool blankets, more tools, a couple of guns, a damp, foxed set of Dickens, several Bibles, and a two-inch stack of $50 Republic of Texas notes. I shoved that damp clump into the side of the backpack. Texas might honor them.

Tools, blankets, clothes, and enough food for a short stay—or until they could get to the exit of the tunnel—seemed to be the focus of those early pioneers. Most of the damp and rotting contents of the boxes were useless to us.

Exhausted, we spread out the blanket and covered it with a small foil solar pad that Mrs. Barnes had packed. I hoped the opportunistic microbes lurking in those old wooden boxes wouldn't target us while we slept.

I COULDN'T SLEEP. Something was targeting me, keeping me awake. This vast, dark, clammy cave so far underground reminded me of the mythological underworld of Annwn in Welsh mythology where hundred-clawed, black-groined toads lurked. In spite of an assortment of monsters, Annwn was considered a kind of paradise of eternal youth. That afterlife would appeal to Mother, no pricey face creams.

I sat upright, thinking of a line about the fabled land of Lyonesse from Tennyson's *Idylls of the King* as I looked at the stacks of old crates—"where fragments of forgotten people dwell."

Beaming my flashlight at the box marked Marchman—Magdalene's ancestors—I wondered if those early settlers had time to examine their pores or worry about wrinkles. The old crates held nothing personal for women—unless they were attached to their skillets—just extra pants and coats for the men.

I flipped on my flashlight, picked up an old pair of wool pants, and shook them with one hand. Helen snored softly on the impossibly hard slab.

Something weighed down one of the pockets. Could it be a coiled viper or a rabid bat? Gingerly, I held the pants up by their cuffs and shook them. A tarnished watch skidded across the stone slab, its crystal reflecting in the dim light.

The faint script "Breguet" on the white face told me all that I needed to know. This was an Eighteenth Century Swiss Silver Quarter Repeater pocket watch. My father and I had admired one at an antique store in Portland. I could clean it up for Magdalene. She'd like that. Maybe this was the watch her great-grandfather couldn't find with his seer stone.

"You're holding that old watch as though you just discovered the Rosetta Stone, Jenny. What's so interesting about it?" Helen asked.

"It's a Breguet. He pioneered the tourbillon. My father and I saw one of his watches once in a high-dollar antique store. Not allowed to touch it." I extended the tarnished treasure on the flat of my hand toward Helen. She didn't look impressed.

"Breguet mounted the escapement, balance spring, and balance wheel within a tiny, rotating cage to fight the effects of gravity. He was trying to achieve accuracy to the second in timekeeping. Magadalene told me her great-grandfather had lost his watch. Now, I've found it!"

Helen nodded affirmatively, the way that a bored parent does to calm an over-eager child. The French tourbillon, whirlwind, wasn't of much interest to a woman who had forgotten her only timepiece, a cheap, digital watch. The balance wheels and hairsprings of a real watch wouldn't intrigue her. Magdalene would understand the effects of gravity better than most. There would have been no free floating with old Cyrus Grund in the house. I curled up next to Helen with the watch clutched in my hand and slept like a baby.

WHEN I WOKE, chilled to the bone, squashed against Helen, I knew what a Stygian night meant to the Greeks. Blacker than black. In the bowels of the earth, time has no meaning where neither the sun nor moon casts light.

I groped for my flashlight. I had no watch. Sleepily, Helen lifted a white arm toward the beam like a lily angling toward light.

"Eleven o'clock, Jenny. I suppose that means it's Sunday. The Sealing Ceremony was scheduled for four o'clock. They've still got a few hours to find us."

I scrabbled around to find the old beeswax candles that Helen had taken out of a crate. They were rock hard but one of them eventually began to burn with a low, wavering flame. "We need to save our batteries. I wasn't able to figure out Mr. Marchman's metrical scale, so I'm not sure how far the tunnel goes. We can count steps until the next turn and make a better guess."

Ignoring me, Helen pulled out the map I had torn out of the old journal and flipped on the small lantern. "I brought one more of these and one of those small wind-up radio and light contraptions that Josh takes camping with him." She held up a small combo device.

"We probably can't get a signal here, but we should be able to recharge the battery. The beeswax smells nice though. We can have breakfast by candlelight. Intimate, don't you think?"

Only if bats and fungi are invited to the party. Surly couldn't begin to describe me when I awoke from sleeping on a decent mattress, never mind atop unyielding bedrock.

For a medium-sized backpack, it held a surprising store: a few apples, several potatoes, a chunk of cheese, a jar of peanut butter, a squashed loaf of bread, a liter of water, a plastic bag of moist hand wipes, and a small framed photograph.

"Josh and his father. It was taken just before the accident." Helen stuttered over the word "accident" as she held up the photo of a smiling Josh and the man he'd look like in twenty years.

Nice. But both of us knew that her husband's death was no accident. Josh had taken some papers when he fled; maybe he had proof of something that could nail the elders for murdering his father.

I had the distinct feeling that I was beginning to grow

moss in the damp chill of the cave. If it were near noon, we needed to move. Even if we reached the end of the tunnel, we might find ourselves in a forest in Canada.

Taking a small swig of water, I passed the bottle to Helen with a warning. "We need to ration the water. Drinking from a stream in the forest made me sick." I couldn't bear to think of the disgusting condition I was in when Josh found me passed out in the forest. Even now, we were probably surrounded by legions of pseudomonas.

"Water purification tablets." Helen held up a small packet of bluish pills. "Best to boil the water too, but I forgot a pot." She wandered over to the pile of rusty and rotting goods we had pilfered from the old crates and picked up a cast-iron skillet flaking rust. "This will work after we clean it."

"Too heavy," I said. "We need to travel light. Save our energy."

"It came out of my ancestors' stores. Our good-luck skillet. We can boil water in it and cook potatoes. You never know when a skillet will come in handy."

I watched her hefting the skillet from hand to hand and thought what a good tool that would have been to smash Jerry's noggin. As it was, he had to go out of this world hearing Toby wailing "how do you like me now" when the boom box shattered his skull. I tried not to think of the instrument of his death as having my hand attached to it.

"At the bend in the tunnel, we follow it left, then straight ahead for some distance." I pushed the fragment of a map into my pocket and crammed everything but the skillet into the backpack. "I'll take the pack. The skillet will weigh you down soon enough."

I thought of Daniel Marchman's account of his wife's prized wardrobe; he had left it by a Joshua tree in a Utah desert—and his unfortunate son nearby beneath a mound of rocks.

Pioneer life must have been beastly difficult, the travelers leaving their families behind and prized possessions along the trail—with one caveat. Those early settlers found a pristine land at the end of their journey, a country unsullied by the native tribes. They should have gloried in such beauty.

Over the years, something went very wrong in the CPRC cult. Maybe all the inbreeding took its toll. With an arch tone, Marybeth cited every relative down to third cousins once removed when I told her we had no other kin—except a missing uncle.

They use genealogy, their so-called racial purity, as a means to establish superiority over others, but it comes back to bite them. Those doltish Bonners walk around with loaded guns in a state of paranoia. A malformed foot ruined a woman's life. Their paradise smelled like Marybeth's rotten egg salad.

The scent of something else rotten rose in the air around us. Just ahead, some large stalactites had broken off the high dome and blocked the main passageway. We skirted to the left for some distance. "Something smells strongly of mold or mildew." Helen stopped and sniffed.

"Worse than that. That's hydrogen sulfide gas. Too much of it can kill us." I flashed the beam ahead where the path narrowed and dropped abruptly out of sight. "Let me go first," I pushed ahead of Helen.

When I aimed the flashlight toward the dark pit ahead,

I gasped. Below us was a huge pool of water with steam rising off it. On the walls above, dozens of stick-like images flickered in the dim light—humans and animals frolicking in perfect harmony.

"The Petroglyphs lead right down to the water. The stones make a kind of shallow ramp into the hot pool. I'm going to take a closer look; the sulfur odor isn't bad," I said, easing my way down the gently sloping incline.

"Careful, Jenny, steam is rising off that water!"

I was too busy peeling off my clothes to pay any attention. Those ancient dancing figures were splashing water and jumping into a steamy pool. It was unlikely that the temperature had changed in all those years. I tested it with a toe, slowly set my foot down, smiled, and eased myself into a small, shallow space for a splendid warm bath.

In the arc of my flashlight, I could see Josh's mother floating on her back like a contented sea otter, her blondish gray hair streaming behind as though she had been transformed into a mythological water nymph. "Anchor your flashlight between the rocks next to mine, Jenny, and come on in. It's wonderful."

"Can't swim," I muttered grumpily, crawling out to shiver on the damp rocks. I could have added that any water over a foot deep terrifies me, but I was leading this little expedition and needed to keep up a veneer of courage.

"I'll teach you. When we get to where we're going, I will teach you to swim, Jenny, my lovely girl. This is a magical place. I haven't had so much fun in ages."

The words of affection and the undisguised pleasure in her voice gave me confidence. The ancient people depicted in Petroglyphs on the sides of this cave found a way in and a way out. We could too. They wouldn't be traveling miles underground just to take a dip.

"I'm refilling our water bottle from the bathtub," Helen said as she dipped the bottle into the hot water. It smells a bit like rotten eggs, but sulfur springs are supposed to be healthy."

CHAPTER 19

Dressed again, we navigated carefully along the narrow edge of the hot springs and came to a gigantic cavern—like photos I'd seen of Carlsbad. I sat down, took out the map. and studied it. "Why wouldn't he have shown this hot springs area or this big cavern?" I asked.

"We might have gone in the wrong direction at that place where the broken stalactites blocked the passage." Helen said—all too calmly in my opinion.

Not only was I chilled to the bone with wet hair, I was feeling a sense of desperation that our little frolic in the water had taken us off the beaten path. We might be hundreds of feet underground without a clue about what lay ahead or behind.

The darkness, the chill, the absolute silence was getting to me. I longed for a sky in one of those Maxfield Parrish paintings where the sun tints the clouds an unreasonable gold.

"We can have a bit of bread and cheese." Helen rustled around in the backpack and pulled out a slab of cheddar and a stiffening loaf of homemade bread.

Handing me a sizeable hunk of cheese and a ragged

piece of bread, she smiled and whispered "Then we'll just follow the yellow brick road."

Feeling too worried to be anything but irritable, I snapped back: "I quit believing in the Wizard along with the tooth fairy long ago. We'll have to backtrack."

She aimed her flashlight ahead of us. On slabs of rocks tumbled end on end like dominos marched a line of stick figures with poles like a milkmaid's yoke. "They carried water out of here. They're showing us the way."

A great, thundering noise rattled from far back in the cave as though hundreds of doors were slamming shut. "I don't think they want us to come back. The roof seems to be caving in back there." I whispered in awe and pulled Helen along at a fast clip.

Within an hour, we came to the mouth of the cave that yawned into a dome of fearless blue, untaxed by a single cloud. On a bluff far above the top of a dense fir forest, Josh's mother and I sat hand-in-hand in the late afternoon sun and meditated, as full of gratitude for our well being as the Dalai Lama.

"I think that might be Lake Pend Oreille way off in the distance, Jenny, but I'm not sure." Helen broke the silence as she stood, stretched, and pointed like Sacagawea showing Lewis and Clark the trail. "I have no idea how to get out of here. It's mostly wilderness. Canada's that way." She pointed northeast. "And Montana's in that direction." She pointed east.

I sent her an uneasy grin. "As long as you can't see the Compound from here, we're home free. What are a few grizzlies and wolves compared to the elders?"

She checked her watch. "It's five o'clock. Time for the ceremony to be over and the feast to begin though I doubt if anyone is celebrating." She glanced at me uneasily. "I'm sorry that we couldn't bring your mother and sister with us. You'll see them soon."

Unless I'm arrested immediately for murder and taken off to Sing-Sing, I thought grimly. The fact that they don't put fifteen-year-olds away with hardened criminals wasn't of much comfort. The elders had their own ways of reprisal. If they could drape their CPA over the horns of a mad bull, a smart-mouthed girl wouldn't stand a chance. My ill feelings overwhelmed me when I thought of the elders. I don't know when my feelings of disgust turned into such hatred. They just did and I had to disguise them with a flippant attitude.

"It might be safer to stay up here on this bluff tonight and try to find our way in the daylight tomorrow. It looks very steep and rocky." Helen wrapped her arms about her body as a brisk wind blasted us. "Katabatic wind. Bad sign. Weather could be coming in. We could go back inside the cave and wait it out."

I wanted off this bluff, through that forest, and to the closest place in civilization I could find as soon as possible. I'd plead rape defense or insanity. Anyone imprisoned in the Compound should be able to plead insanity. "I don't trust those people with Mother and Lorena. I want them out of there."

"Most of our people are good, Christian, hard-working folks. They wouldn't harm anyone. Some zealots have gotten the upper hand. That's too bad." Helen's face flushed as though "too bad" was a gross understatement of the facts.

Murder, rape, forced marriages, sex with underage girls, kidnapping, drugging and theft. I could go on and on naming the sins of the elders and their sons, but it wouldn't get us any closer to civilization or make Helen despise the elders as much as I did.

"Let's try that narrow trail off to the left. I think we can climb down these rocks. If we get into the woods by dark, we can make some kind of shelter. Maybe a fire to roast those potatoes we've been lugging around?" I asked, trying to be upbeat.

Getting off the bluff took two hours of zigzagging along layers of rocks, running into dead ends, and searching for footholds down to the next layer. A six-foot drop left us panting on a thick thatch of fir needles that led into an impenetrable forest.

Helen was in her element, as preachy as I am when geometry or clock works are mentioned. She snatched at branches of overhanging trees and named them: "Western white pine. Red cedar. And subalpine fir. In the same vicinity. Odd."

Not to me. They all looked like the Douglas fir that put a barrier between the Compound and the rest of the world.

"Sitka and chokecherry." She thumbed some berries. "I can make such good jam out of these."

I glowered back at her. We were not on a berry picking expedition. Our water supply was low, and I was never going to drink water in a forest again. Not even with little blue purification tablets. Never.

Without the sun to cast any shadows or the moon visible above, we might just as well have been in the cave again.

"It's getting cold, Helen. We need some kind of shelter for the night." I had spotted a five-foot high stub of an old tree with the trunk still attached that formed a perfect isosceles triangle with the ground. We could anchor fir branches along the side of the downed trunk for shelter if only I had any rope.

Hareton Earnshaw, Heath's darling twelve-year-old brother, had provided the solution. With a bit of regret, I took a knife to the hot pink paracord survival bracelet that Hareton had proudly made for me and stretched out about nine feet of cord.

Breaking off fir branches indiscriminately, I piled them stems up against the trunk and lashed them down with the paracord. We wouldn't be protected from bears or wolves or a downpour, but badgers and porcupines might leave us alone.

Within minutes, Helen had cleared the site of fir needles, piled up dead branches, and started a fire. Pulling out a small square of foil from the backpack, she wrapped four potatoes and buried them under the coals.

We sat by a blazing fire and felt oddly comforted by the warmth—as though our trial were almost over. I knew that mine had really just begun. Mother and Lorena were still in lockdown, just as I would be when Jerry's body was found.

I blocked out everything but our feast. Baked potatoes without sour cream, slathers of butter, salt, and pepper were scrumptious. Near starvation, an icy night, and a foreboding forest gave those potatoes a piquancy that was unimaginably delicious.

With our heads locked together on the pillow of a

lumpy backpack, we gazed up through the thatch of fir branches overhead at a smattering of stars.

"That's the Corona Borealis. The crown that Ariadne, daughter of King Minos of Crete, wore at her wedding." The voice of Helen was soft in the fir-fresh forest as she named other constellations that we couldn't see through the overhead branches.

But, I was remembering Ariadne and the ball of thread she gave Theseus to find his way out of the labyrinth after he had killed the monstrous Minotaur. String saved Theseus just as the survival bracelet Hareton made for me helped protect us this night.

Reading Greek mythology had always been a delight for me. I wandered into my own thoughts as Helen talked softly of stars. Theseus had two fathers: Aegeus and Poseidon. His mother Aethra slept with both in one night. (When I thought of Heath and Josh, I admired her style.)

I had only one father—but a look-alike uncle, Mother's original fiancé. Back then, girls waited on a ceremony, so she probably didn't sleep with my father's identical twin. She certainly cohabited with Gomer Darken. Those Monolo Blahnik snakeskin heels don't come cheap.

"The Pleiades, Jenny. See them up there?" Helen pointed through the fir branches, interrupting my dark thoughts of Mother and her shoes. "Some people call them the seven sisters."

I remembered them now—sisters with a single father, Atlas carrying heaven on his back. Sisters, not sisterwives—the wives of greedy men who make their wives call each other sister while they're busy hating each other's guts.

The Pleiades sisters committed suicide. Nice if Marybeth would read a little mythology and follow suit.

The night seemed very long with sporadic showers that seeped through our makeshift shelter, waking me periodically to half-remembered nightmares. Wind soughing through fir branches should sooth the dreams of tired sleepers. I finally fell into an exhausted sleep to the rhythm of Helen's snores.

CHAPTER 20

Just at sunrise, the crashing of branches, the drum of boots on fallen logs, and soft whispers told me that the enemy had found us. Something panting and furry tasted my cheek. *Freeze when a bear attacks.* I dared not open my eyes.

"Jenny? Jenny? Are you OK?" The boyishly smooth cheek of Hareton plastered itself against my upturned face.

"She's here! She's fine! So's Josh's mother! Pip found them!" The shrieks of Hareton might have carried all the way to the Compound had I not flung myself around him in a life-affirming grip.

Just like the dancing princess Sue Ann with her octopus squeeze that day in the Earnshaw kitchen, I clung. I remembered Hareton pushing her away with annoyance. This Hareton clung to me as though I had returned from the underworld. I had.

One side of our fir-branch shelter moved slightly, revealing a morning full of shadowy figures. "Let her breathe, Hareton. You and that dog are crushing her." Framed by fir branches on the side of the shelter, Heathcliff's gorgeous face chased away the fog of nightmares.

Pip, the wolfdog I had saved from a spring trap out in the forest on the Res, pushed Hareton aside as I sat up and slathered my face with doggy licks.

As Heath pulled me to my feet, I saw Josh kneeling beside his mother and whispering softly as though she might shatter from the sound of a normal voice. Or they might be sharing secrets. I stood up and stretched, silent with relief that some of my nightmares had ended.

At that moment, Hareton reached into his waistband, pulled out something that looked lethal and shot a screaming flare into the air.

"For God's sake, Hareton. You'll burn down the forest with that thing. Give it here!" Heath snatched at the flare gun, but Hareton dodged his brother.

"Hal told me to use it if I needed to," he said defensively. "Pip and I found them. That lady gave us good clues." Hareton nodded with a pleased-as-punch look at Helen and me and continued. "If I hadn't been listening on my shortwave, we might never have . . ."

"What lady?" Helen asked.

"That Magdalene lady. She's a ham operator, like me. She said she saw both of you two nights ago running through some bushes near her house. Then, you just disappeared. Like you'd fallen off the edge of the earth, she said. She said if she was running, she'd head to a state park like Farragut and stay off main roads . . . and something about Romans that didn't make any sense."

It just dawned on me that Hareton said his flare gun was my Uncle Hal's, my don't-give-a-damn-about-my-family uncle who didn't offer to help rescue Lorena and Mother.

Just over a week ago, Heath, Hareton and I had gone on a wild goose chase to the south coast of Oregon to find my missing uncle. A few hours later, Jerry nabbed me in a Spokane alley and hauled me back to the Compound.

Before I could work myself into a tizzy about a blood uncle who denied his own kin, my feet left the ground and whipped around in a circle as someone stronger than Hareton crushed me against his chest.

"Jenny. Jenny. Jenny. You ran off from my house without even giving me a chance to help you. I am so frustrated that I'd strangle you if I weren't so relieved to see you."

He was strangling me. In the nicest, most affectionate way that I could imagine. Uncle Hal's eyes welled with tears. He flushed with embarrassment, stood me on my feet, and then pulled me next to him again.

"You and Lorena—and Clara—are the only family I have. Why wouldn't I help? Seeing you was a shock. I needed time to get my sea legs. I wasn't even sure if bigamy was a felony in Oregon. It is. A Class C felony," he said grimly to no one in particular as he turned me to face him.

"Luckily, Heath left his phone number, so I called the Earnshaw house the minute I returned to find you and the boys had gone. When Heath called his folks to report that you had disappeared in Spokane, they contacted me immediately."

He clapped Heath on the shoulder with the same friendly familiarity he had shown both boys on his boat—the instant bonding that had so annoyed me. "Heath checked with people that had booths in the Farmers Market and found out that the CPRC group had folded their tent and left. We assumed they'd taken you. You're home free now."

Not exactly, but I couldn't bear to spoil the moment. Hareton looked so pleased with himself. Heath's smile dazzled this foggy morning. Even Uncle Hal seemed a bit overwrought from all his high-spirited hugging.

I looked over at Josh and his mother. Helen stood flushed with happiness. Maybe I should cushion the blow. They'd know soon enough that I was wanted for murder. I'd start my defense with the unvarnished truth about Jerry Winner.

"Jerry put a chokehold on me in an alley. He said he learned it from watching Jack Reacher in *24 Hours*. Jack drops his victims so neatly that they recover without any ill effects." I rubbed my neck. No one seemed to appreciate my digression. I'd get to the point.

"Jerry and Enoch Bonner with three women hauled me back to the Compound. In front of a crowd at the gate of the Compound, I decked one of them, my so-called stepmother Marybeth, so Enoch dislocated my shoulder. About a week later, Jerry tricked me into meeting him at the Honeymoon Retreat and throttled me again."

I was too humiliated to continue. Murder doesn't hold a candle to stupidity. I should have known Mother didn't write that note or that Marybeth would give me a note from a woman she despised.

Helen moved away from Josh and flung her arms around me. "Jenny was attacked by Jerry. She hit him in self-defense. She had no other option but to defend herself."

Like a crafty lawyer, Helen was setting forth a defense

before the enormity of the crime was exposed. We didn't need to belabor the point about two enforced marriages that we had narrowly escaped.

At that moment, Bill Earnshaw with his wolfdog Raven came crashing through the underbrush toward us and shouted: "I saw the flare. Knew something had happened. Thank God, both of you are OK." He gave me a quick hug and turned to Helen.

"Too long, Helen. It's been far too long. Josh told us about what the elders were trying to do. What they probably did to . . ." He reached for her hand and held it for one long moment as though the unspoken words about her husband were a silent communion between two old friends.

I didn't want to be the one to extinguish the blaze of his smile—or the quizzical expression on my Uncle Hal's face, but I had to do it. Murder will out as Chaucer reminded us. A clever murderer wouldn't have left such a clear trail behind— bloodstained clothes in Helen's house and fingerprints on the murder weapon.

"I didn't just hit him. I cracked his skull open with a boom box. It was playing Toby Keith," I added, sadly, not really wanting to make Toby complicit in my crime. "I murdered him."

"You saved yourself, Jenny. You don't know that you . . ." Helen stood between our rescuers and me as though our friends might haul me off to jail at any moment.

"That thick-headed troglodyte had it coming." Josh flashed those dimples at me as Heath grinned over my head at him.

"You split his head open, and he bled like a stuck pig.

He's still explaining to his father why he was in the Retreat wearing only his skivvies. Marybeth found him." Heath patted my shoulder. "She said you were a Jezebel. I hope so." He winked as Josh scowled at him.

I looked at Heath and Josh questioningly. "How do you ..."

"Someone from the Compound gave Ebon Riley a heads up that you were on the lam, armed and dangerous, having assaulted an innocent boy. Ebon came poking around the house to see what we knew. Ma pried the information out of him."

Heath and I locked eyes uneasily. We both suspected that Ebon was complicit in the dancing princess's hit and run death—and that he was probably the father of her unborn child. Tribal Police business, Aunt Izzy had warned us. She said they might move slowly but believed like the Romans that justice will give each his due.

CHAPTER 21

Driving with Uncle Hal in the front of his pickup toward the Earnshaws, Martin Luther King's Dream Speech echoed in my head: "Great God Almighty, free at last!"

Aunt Izzy stood on the front porch, waving her arms. Behind her I could see Gramps, looking a bit like Iron Eyes Cody weeping for the planet. The youngest Earnshaw, Cathy, ran alongside the pickup shouting: "Jenny! Jenny! I knew they'd find you."

"I found her, Cathy. Me. The great tracker. Pip and me." Hareton shouted from the open window from his dad's jeep and running over to claim one side of me as I headed toward the porch.

Two more men stood in the shadows, shifting from foot to foot like clumsy dancers, searching for the beat before they ventured onto the floor.

"Mr. Tomeh!" I shouted. This was the man who had helped me with Pip when I found him injured in the forest.

A man who looked enough like him to be his twin stepped out. "Remember me, Jenny?"

I did. It was the other Mr. Tomeh, the man who used to

sleep on the sidewalk vent outside our crummy apartment in Portland, the man to whom we sometimes carried food on a paper plate—with Mother warning us not to talk to strangers.

"Ed came to Portland and found me. I have you to thank for that, Jenny. I'm in your debt."

This sober, happy man looked nothing like the man Mr. Darken had kicked away from the door when he hauled Mother, Lorena and me away from our apartment to "clean air, good friends, and paradise."

This little reunion might be as close to paradise as I would ever come. Long-separated brothers stood side by side; Aunt Izzy and Helen clutched each other like long-lost sisters; Heath and Josh jabbed at each other, dodging blows, in that male bonding thing that boys seem to love; Raven and Pip nipped each other; and Uncle Hal and my adopted grandfather, "Gramps," patted me on the back as though I'd just won a 10K.

"We have to go back!" My screech unnerved even me. "I can't be happy when Mother and Lorena are still in the Compound. I almost killed Elder Winner's son. Who knows what he might do for revenge." It wasn't a question. No one had an answer. Then Aunt Izzy did.

"Into the kitchen. All of you. Not the dogs. Out!" She shoved Raven and Pip back from the door. "Breakfast has been ready for almost an hour. We can talk better over food."

Before I could protest, Aunt Izzy drew me tightly against her. "We've been tossing around ideas for several days, ever since Josh got here. Whew!" She sniffed my hair. "You smell of sulfur."

"We've been in the bowels of the earth, caves as big

and beautiful as you can imagine. We took a little dip in a hot sulfur pool." *Actually, Helen took a dip. I cowered in shallow water near the edge.*

"Spelunkers." The word came softly into the room as Ed Tomeh stepped forward. "My brother and me. When we were boys, we spent more time underground than on top of it. We can help."

"We have an old map, but we must have missed a turn when we had to detour around a blocked passage. Just before we left the cave, we could hear a tremendous thundering, as though the entire thing was collapsing behind us. It may be sealed," I said, feeling a bit hopeless.

"Happens sometimes. Calcium salts build up on stalactites, and they break off like icicles. Make a terrific noise. Those chambers echo. If you got through, so can we." Mr. Tomeh's brother chimed in.

The voice of reason came through loud and clear as Bill Earnshaw stepped forward: "I have no doubt. Getting into the Compound underground is an option, but we need to consider every possibility, including the police and legal avenues. I talked to a colleague of mine who used to be with the FBI just after you disappeared in Spokane, Jenny. The kidnapping angle," he nodded soberly at me.

"He said the FBI is very reluctant to force their way into one of these compounds. The Waco siege with the Branch Davidians caused bad publicity for the Bureau. He was doubtful that they would intervene. Sorry to disappoint you, Jenny, but he said on the surface it appears that Gomer Darken married a woman with two underage children and took them to his home. The police . . ."

I interrupted: "Bigamy is a Class C felony in Oregon. Uncle Hal said so. Gomer Darken already had two wives. Maylene told me that she and Mr. Darken were legally married in West Virginia before moving to the Compound." I was trying to make a retort as calmly as possible, but the steam was rising.

"I have been strangled twice by Jerry and tied up like a trussed turkey while he . . ." *I couldn't think rationally about that red bedspread, the white cords on my wrists and ankles, and his horseradish appendage. Time to spread the blame.*

"Enoch Bonner dislocated my shoulder. Mr. Darken and the elders drugged me and locked me in an attic. Where does assault and battery fit into the Bureau's *reluctance* to get involved?"

"Sorry, Jenny. You're right to be angry. We haven't contacted the Bureau officially. I was just trying to get a feel for the best way to proceed. What legal grounds we might use." Bill flushed with embarrassment.

"Legally is not the way." Helen's low voice cut through the tension I had caused with my little diatribe. "Jenny omitted two murders: my husband and Abigail Johnson. The elders answer only to the Council. Legal structures lie outside their way of thinking," she said, looking like a disgruntled schoolmarm whose students were giving her wrong answers.

"If they get wind of any kind of police or federal interference, Lorena will be taken away to another Compound in another Ward and lost forever. We need to act as soon as possible. Mr. Darken and his wives can disappear immediately. Clara too." Helen gazed across the table at Uncle Hal, as though she might be assessing his level of commitment to my mother.

Josh stepped forward and put his arm around his mother. "Mom's right. The Compound has become like one of those third world military states where the potential of outside interference increases paranoia. Even the younger boys are carrying guns."

"Then, we'll have to outwit them." Bill's burst of confidence startled me. "We could create some kind of disturbance at the front gate—make it official. Tribal concerns."

He looked over at Gramps. "Couldn't you get a few men from the Tribal Council to join us? Surely we have some grievances. They've been overgrazing our land for years—one cow and calf for twenty acres. That was our agreement. Their misuse is blatant. We can take Ebon with us."

"But he's a . . ." I was just about to stutter out "murderer" when Heath's father said quietly. "Yes. I know. Many of us know. That might make him more cooperative. He's thick as thieves with the elders and Darken. We have a better chance of getting close with him among us."

Heath edged forward. "Timing is critical. If Josh and I could get through the tunnel, we could figure out how to get Jenny's sister and mother back to the tunnel without causing an alarm. We know the Compound layout."

"I've got a better idea," Ed Tomeh spoke up again. "Two distractions—one at the front and one on the grounds. Two spelunkers all suited up for cave exploration just happen to emerge into the Compound. Who's going to be alarmed by two old men? We case the joint while the tribal members keep the guards busy at the gate."

"Case the joint? You've been reading too many old crime novels, Ed. These people are dangerous. They carry Uzis. Your head lamps won't be much of a threat." Aunt Izzy's voice was soothing, even though I thought her words were somewhat offensive.

So did Ed Tomeh. He ruffled like a fighting cock. "My brother and I owe Jenny. We're going in."

"Me too!" shouted Hareton into his mother's frowning face.

"I'm not staying behind. Not me! Not this time!" Cathy joined the fray.

"May I have the floor?" Uncle Hal's voice boomed like a bass drum. He wasn't asking. "We're talking about guerilla warfare. Any of you ever been involved in a rescue operation?"

The silence in the room was awkward, including lots of shuffling of feet.

"I have. On the coast. Central America. Pirates took some of our crew in a little village. We got them back. Some casualties. Not ours."

With a kind of Hugh Jackman in-your-face ambiance, Uncle Hal held the attention of everyone in the room. "When I listen to Jenny and Helen and Josh, who know the people in the Compound best, I realize that urgency is critical and a covert action our only option. Not the police or FBI. We can't trust anyone but the people in this room."

"Hareton, Cathy. If you two will serve as my first lieutenants, I'd like you to post yourselves on the porch and let us know immediately if anyone is coming this way. Take the dogs with you."

I almost smiled as Hareton leaped to attention and pulled Cathy uncomplaining out the door.

"The first rule of a covert action is clear purpose. That means we plan carefully, move with tactical speed and keep in touch every step of the way with two-way radios. It's probably too remote for our cell phones."

"It's too remote for any phones except the ones that the elders keep to themselves." I interrupted snidely. "We just need to get in at night and back out through the tunnel." I glanced at Helen for affirmation. The men seemed to be running this show.

"They do have land-line phones, since the 1960s. Every house has one, but some of the men restrict their women from using them. That's why Magdalene uses her father's old short wave. She has other ham contacts out there. We might be able to reach her, but certainly not by phone. That's locked in Cyrus's office."

"An instrument of the devil, huh? Like lip gloss and the Internet?" No one seemed amused by my effort to break the mounting tension.

I tried again. "I'm just pointing out that Josh, his mother, and I know the territory and the people who are most dangerous."

"And they know each of you," Uncle Hal said grimly. "I don't think that you three should go near the Compound. If the Tomeh brothers can help me through the tunnel, they can wait inside while I find Lorena and Clara."

Tull Tomeh muttered: "You will recognize Clara, but you don't know Lorena. I do. The girls brought me food sometimes. I watched Jenny and Lorena and their mother coming and going to their apartment in Portland every day for a year—until that man took them away."

Just as Uncle Hal was about to protest, Tull's spine stiffened. "I may look old and helpless, but I know how to be invisible. Years of living on the street can . . ." His voice trailed off as he seemed to be in the grip of an internal struggle. "Gomer Darken kicked me when he ran off with the girls and their mother. I don't forget that kind of thing."

"Me neither." I snatched up his hand and held it firmly in mine. "I can get us through that cave."

"You can't go, Jenny. I'm not a demonstrative man, but I should have expressed more concern when you and the boys showed up in Charleston. I felt it. I just was in such a state of shock that I couldn't react the way I should have. I won't put you at risk again. You and your family are my responsibility." Uncle Hal eyed me resolutely.

Uncle Hal telling me what I could and couldn't do would have riled me in the past. At this moment, I was melting with affection for this take-charge uncle of mine.

"That's it then. Josh and Helen can draw us a complete plan of the Compound. Heath, you go locate some of radios we use at digs. Ed and his brother will go through the tunnel with you, Hal. I'll go with Gramps and his crew to cause a distraction at the front gate. Restricting grazing rights will get their attention." Bill raised his voice above the hubbub to restore order, ticking off tasks on one hand.

He seemed as enthusiastic as though he might be orchestrating a new archeological dig on the Compound. Finding old bones is not quite the same as coming across someone firing ten bullets a second at you, but I didn't want to dampen his eagerness to help.

"I have a gun in my pickup. I'll take that. I have a conceal/carry license for Oregon that's valid in Idaho."

Uncle Hal seemed to be on my wavelength. Be prepared to gun them down.

"I wouldn't take any firearms to the gate. The disturbance there should be just an argument about the grazing rights they're abusing." Uncle Hal looked at Gramps soberly, as though he thought another round of the Indian Wars might be in the offing.

"This discussion about guns isn't moving us along," Helen said quietly. "We need to scout out the territory. Find out when the elders might be away at a Council meeting. Mr. Darken goes to the Council meetings as well. It would be best to act when he's away. You don't want to run into him." She sent a particularly piercing glance my way.

"If I can borrow your sentry Hareton, Mr. Hatchet, Hareton and I will try to rouse Magdalene on his shortwave. She's a particular friend of Jenny's. We can trust her."

Helen smiled across at Uncle Hal, a smile so piqued with interest that I noted Josh's sudden frown. Best to create another diversion.

"It took Helen and me about two days to get through the tunnel. I'll mark the map and try to pinpoint where we made a detour and found the sulfur springs. The way in and out of there is clearly marked with Petroglyphs."

"Petroglyphs?" Bill whirled toward me. "In the tunnel?" The enthusiasm on his face could derail our plans quickly.

"They've probably been there for hundreds of years,

Bill. They'll be waiting for you after we finish the business at hand." Aunt Izzy rubbed his arm soothingly. "I feel confident that Ed, Tull, and Hal can get in and out of that place quickly and safely. "I do need to pack food and blankets for the return trip with Clara and Lorena. They'll probably be traveling light."

Yeah, I thought grimly. *With a kitten, if I knew my sister, and a suitcase full of shoes unless my mother had undergone a transmogrification.*

CHAPTER 22

By early afternoon, the preparations were done. The Tomeh brothers' caving gear—helmets, headlamps, ropes, carabiners, and waterproof clothes—had been stuffed into their backpacks. An assortment of MRE portables cluttered the kitchen table as Josh and Heath explained its use to the skeptical spelunkers.

"Beef jerky worked just fine when we explored in our younger days," Ed said huffily. "I guess Jenny's mother and sister might not care for it."

Nope, I thought. Lorena calls it Egyptian mummy meat.

By mid-afternoon, Helen had roused Magdalene on the shortwave. She came into the kitchen and announced that the Ward Council meeting was near Boise—two days away. Gomer Darken and all the elders but Elder Grund would go.

"Magdalene said Cyrus is still having episodes with his heart. She sounded almost gleeful. She said Elder Winner is on the rampage. He's telling everyone that Jenny lured his son into the Honeymoon Retreat just to humiliate him."

"Like I tied myself to the bedposts and exposed his chicken legs for entertainment." I scowled at everyone. *I didn't mention the root of the matter.*

"Magdalene will be on the lookout with her telescope for our men coming out of the tunnel and distract anyone who might be in the area." Helen looked quizzically at me.

"She said something rather odd. She said she'd give away her fortune just to watch the fireworks when the men get Clara and Lorena out through the tunnel—but she's already given it to her best friend. You think she meant those rings she gave you, Jenny? They're probably worth a great deal, but if Cyrus hadn't taken her property for himself, Magdalene would be the largest landowner in the Compound."

Time to come clean. "I have her will and the deed to her land, a signature card for her bank account—lots of other papers she gave me. Fifty-fifty. Josh and me."

Josh interrupted: "You have got to be kidding. Why would she . . ."

"Magdalene said I'm her best friend and she's very fond of you. She's leaving you her Steinway. I have her rings." I blushed. Here I was blithely explaining away a fortune I didn't deserve while the woman who owned it was caged inside the Compound.

"I don't want her property. I want to go with you guys and get Magdalene out. But Helen says she won't come," I added morosely.

"Mom's right. Magdalene loves that land her great-grandfather claimed. There should be a way to legally restore it to her. And Dad's property to Mom. That carpetbagger Simmons family has no right to be in our house. They may have paid the Council for it, but I took our deeds when I rode out of that place. It appears we both need legal advice."

Josh was staring at me with new interest. *Could it be that an heiress is more interesting than a 10K runner?*

Uncle Hal stood up abruptly. "These are issues we can discuss later. Ed, we need to go now. If the elders are leaving in two days for a daylong meeting, we've got a narrow time frame. We can drive into the forest where we found Jenny and Helen, but we have to hike to that bluff—and get to the top of it. Who knows what we'll find inside the cave or how long we'll be in it."

"Go. Take my jeep. It's got an extra row of seats," Heath's father said as he started lugging backpacks out the door. In minutes, Uncle Hal had disappeared with the only map I had of the tunnel.

Identical scowls formed on the faces of Josh and Heath as they muttered in unison: "We know the territory. They don't."

Quick as Pip when it came to sniffing out bad moods, I needed to use their disappointment to my advantage.

Aunt Izzy beat me to it. "You boys should be useful. Heath, take Josh up to the lake and see if you can snag some salmon. I'll have the smoker fired up. Jenny, why don't you go with them? Helen and I are going to do some baking."

I had bad memories of the place where Cathy had perversely ignored me and cut her leg. And, being in a boat in deep water gave me the willies. "I'll just stay here and play with Pip. I've missed him."

Tossing the Frisbee to Pip wasn't working. I was more pissed off than Heath or Josh. I should be at the center of this drama. Not on the sidelines. It was my family at risk. Josh and his mother were safe.

Mulishly, I thought about Edgar Allen Poe's description of perversity in "The Black Cat," a story you'd never want to read at night. He called it the "unfathomable longing of the soul to vex itself." I'd call it my middle name. Jenny Perverse Hatchet.

The spirit of perversity was settling on me even while I was feeling remorse for it. If I couldn't be a participant in the action, I could have a front-row seat. I knew that Heath and Josh shared my frustration.

Within an hour Heath pulled his old jeep into the drive and shouted: "They ain't biting, Ma." Bad grammar and calling his mother "Ma" would double her irritation.

I trotted over to the jeep. "I think that we should take your jeep and drive as close to the bluff as possible. Camp out nearby. They might find a short cut through that cave and get out sooner than planned. Or some of those loonies might follow them. We should be there just in case."

Josh stared at me quietly as though he were trying to make up his mind, then nodded and grinned with all his dimples on display so that zing went the strings of my . . .

"Great idea," Heath interrupted my brief reverie. "They might need backup. My camping stuff is in the garage. Won't take me a minute to load it. Jenny, why don't you go work on Mom and Helen. Tell them you've never been camping with real gear. You can play them like a fiddle. Nab some food."

Watching Heath and Josh grinning at each other, I realized how much I adored both of them. Not in that mad sweep-me-off my feet kind of passion in romance novels. Just a hollow sense of loneliness when they weren't around.

I wondered if Jerry Winner had put the kibosh on the dubious pleasures of violation by the opposite sex. His gangly legs and lumpy boxer shorts had really put me off.

It wasn't just the fact that both Heath and Josh could vie for the cover of *Vogue* with Eddie Redmayne—the same not-so-innocent handsome face—I really did enjoy their company.

We liked the same music—Coldplay, Lucinda Williams and Mozart. We laughed at the same things. My time seemed more precious around them.

As they came out of the garage, tossing bags back and forth, exhibiting the rough and tumble of friends who have missed each other but can't say so, I realized that what I was feeling for them wasn't the kind of sexual tension that keeps Harlequin heroines on the grocery store racks.

When I remembered Josh carrying me through the forest to safety after my first escape and recalled how Heath held me so quietly after Helen and I had cut and run again, I realized their impulse was to protect me.

Since my father had died, no one else had done that for me. It might be love that I was feeling for them or just gratitude. I was fifteen years old. For now, that was enough to feel.

At this moment, I just wanted to get on with my life—that meant in the same location with Mother and Lorena. I needed to finish high school, run more 10Ks, and go to a university. Otherwise, Mother might find someone else to buy her shoes. Maybe she and Uncle Hal. No, not my father's identical twin. I didn't like the sound of that. Smacked of necrophilia or incest.

Living in the Compound had done one thing for me. My sense of outrage for those worn-out, ground-down women had been honed razor sharp. Some of those women might have once had a passion for someone or some thing, but it couldn't endure in a place where choice is proscribed.

The cheerful sound of feminine voices struck me as I entered the kitchen. Helen was sketching new designs for her pottery; she and Aunt Izzy were discussing Isabel Archer, Henry James' heroine who made a bad choice in men. Neither of these women had.

At the end, I had to live my life, not disappear into someone else's life. Subservient to a man's career. Practicing little domestic economies for faint praise. Or, like Mother, not practicing them at all, and inadvertently sending her husband off to drown in a river. Dependence is a dreadful thing—and, Mother was a born dependent.

"We're going camping just by the lake for a couple of days—get our minds off what might be happening at the Compound." I tossed off the decision as though there wasn't a dependent bone in my body.

From the skeptical expression on Aunt Izzy's face, she wasn't buying it. Helen countered sympathetically. "Of course, Jenny. That's a good idea. All this waiting around is unnerving. Open air heals the spirit. Can I pack food for them, Izzy?"

CHAPTER 23

As we bumped along beside the lake on the way to the bluff, Heath flipped on the radio. Toby Keith belted out "You Shouldn't Kiss Me Like This" as I revisited that nightmare in the Retreat with Jerry.

"Could we hear *anything* else? It isn't Toby's fault, but Jerry used his CD as background music for attempted rape."

"Sorry, Jenny. We only get AM in this part of the area. No music. We'll just concentrate on getting this old wreck as far into the forest as we can. Then backpack the rest of the way." For once, Heath looked disturbingly sober, as though he had made a faux pas.

ROUGH CAMPING WITH the right equipment was a civilized pastime, especially when someone else set up tents, unrolled sleeping bags, and did all the cooking.

We were able to drive to within 500 yards of the animal path that Helen and I had taken from the bluff. With binoculars, we could almost make out a dark smudge on the bluff. That would be the cave entrance.

I felt like one of those prized concubines from the

Trojan War, either Briseis or Chryseis. My Achilles and Agamemnon were doing their dead-level best to keep me from thinking about the war that might be going on back at the Compound with stupid card games. If I never play gin rummy again, it will be too soon.

"ONE MORE NIGHT, then we're going in," I pronounced grimly. "Something must have happened."

"Give them until tomorrow morning—then we'll go in, Jenny. They have a good plan. Dad, Gramps, and his friends on the Tribal Council are threatening to take away the Compound's grazing rights. That should get their attention. Your Uncle Hal seems to know what he's doing. If we get in the middle of his covert operation, he won't like it." Heath sounded almost apologetic.

Clear purpose. A single command. Tactical speed. I had heard Uncle Hal reviewing the plan as though he were Che Guevera mobilizing his guerillas. Two old guys who explored caves in their younger days—and some quarrelsome men from the Res at the gates. Some plan. I'd give them until sunup, then I was heading back into the tunnel, plan be damned.

AS THE SUN god Ra on his boat of a million years headed into the underworld, we sat around our campfire too worried to talk as the forest darkened in a slanting light.

The noise of a pickup and Gramp's shout simultaneously broke the silence: "I told Izzy this is where they'd be. Camping by the lake my foot. I didn't believe that for a minute. She said you had your cell phone, Heath, but she couldn't reach you."

Gramps eased his rangy body out of the pickup and gave us a canny look. "We got more action than we expected at the gate of the Compound. In a flash, he was gone."

"Mother and Lorena," I whispered, fearing the worst, visualizing Gomer Darken speeding away with my mother and sister, never to be found again. I could feel my heart fracturing—not a clean break, but a fracture that would take forever to heal.

"They're fine, Jenny. Should be coming out of the cave any time. We lost radio contact with your uncle and the Tomeh brothers after they went back into the cave." Heath's father checked his watch. "That was about eighteen hours ago."

Gramps threw his arm around me. "Slick as molasses. They got through the tunnel up on the bluff and made it out just where you said, by the blackberry vines near the Grund house. Your little sister just happened to be visiting your mother at the Darken house—they were outside on the porch with her cat."

Chuckling, Gramps said: "Hal said one of those sisterwives made a terrible racket when she saw three strange men outside."

"Marybeth."

He nodded. "Hal had to put duct tape on her mouth and tie her up. The other one called Maylene helped your mother grab a few things. Slowed them down a bit. Shoes, I think she said. Odd."

Relief flooded over me. On the deck of the Titanic, Mother would argue with the deckhands about fitting her shoes into a lifeboat. Some irritating habits can be very comforting.

"What kind of action is Gramps talking about, Dad?" Heath's concern caused Josh to look edgy.

"One casualty. Elder Grund. He got out of his sick bed when one of the guards went up to his house to tell him that tribal officials were at the gate and needed to talk to someone in charge." Bill shook his head. "He was in no . . ."

Gramps interrupted. "Damned near messed up our plan. Hal and the Tomehs were just coming out of the cave behind the house when the guard drove up to get Elder Grund. If some crazy woman hadn't been screaming out a window and distracted the guard, they'd have been caught for sure."

"Cyrus Grund's heart simply gave out. The minute he stepped out of the guard's car, he tumbled over," Heath's father said. "One of the guards tried to resuscitate him for half an hour."

"She showed up," Gramps said in a puzzled way. "That wife of Cyrus Grund. Someone fetched her when they couldn't bring him around. Poor woman limps worse than I do. She didn't touch him. She just looked at him and said the weirdest thing." He shook his head.

"What?" Josh and I shouted together.

"'Troy has fallen. She gores his fenceless side,'" Bill answered. "I asked Izzy. She said it's what Cassandra says in that Greek play when Clytemnestra stabs her husband."

He looked down at his feet. "We didn't expect anything

like that to happen. Just a clean get-away for Jenny's mother and sister. As soon as we knew they had made it to the tunnel, we just sort of faded away. I'm sorry that happened."

"I'm not." Josh's voice was harsh. "Elder Grund supervised the dairy operation. A dairy bull killed my father. Grund made Magdalene's life miserable and intended to add my mother to his harem. I hope he rots in hell." His voice cracked with emotion.

Surprised by Josh's fury, I looked over at Heath. The expression on his face was almost beatific—or it might have been ghoulish depending on the light.

"Confucius said we should recompense injury with justice and recompense kindness with kindness. Maybe justice has been served." Heath said to no one in particular.

"And we will find some way to repay Magdalene for everything she's done for us," I added, louder than I intended.

Almost as loud as the shrill treble voice echoing across the tops of a vast fir forest: "Jenny! Jenny! Jenny!"

Way off in the distance, on the edge of the bluff, I could see Uncle Hal with a child on his shoulders and the Tomeh brothers supporting a stumbling woman.

Only Mother would attempt spelunking in four-inch heels.. Life was resuming normalcy at an amazing speed.

CHAPTER 24

Two months later

Rubbing Pip's ears while we sat on the pier in Charleston waiting for Uncle Hal and Helen, I thought about Argo, the faithful dog that Odysseus left behind for so many years. Old, sick, and neglected, Argo recognized his disguised master when he returned but could only lift his head. Odysseus dared not respond, so Argo died of grief.

My good friend Pip and I stared across a velvety gray sea, a troubled shade for such a promising, sunny day. Pip, who could always trust me to acknowledge him, paced off a perfect circle, dropped his head onto my knees, and drifted into a shallow sleep that let me know Uncle Hal's boat would soon appear on the horizon.

I thought back to the morning after Mother and Lorena were rescued. A soft tapping on my door at Aunt Izzy's woke me way too early. Mother and Lorena were twisted in a snarl of blankets on my bed. I had opted for an air mattress on the floor.

"Phone call for you Jenny. From the Compound." Aunt Izzy whispered through a crack in the door.

Magdalene's snaggletooth whisper had a jubilant lilt, but I could hardly make out her words. "Can you speak louder, Magdalene?"

"Sorry, Jenny. We get in the habit of whispering around here. I said that Cyrus has been stashed in the frozen food locker. They're planning a big service next week. I'm not going." Her voice was emphatic.

"Helen called last night to let me know that both of you made it out safely—and your mother and sister are back with you. I'm vastly relieved. I thought you'd be pleased by a morsel of information about the Darken household."

I waited silently. Anything less than a public beheading of Gomer Darken wouldn't give me the sense of revenge I craved after seeing Mother, vacant-eyed and stumbling out of that tunnel.

"The elders and Gomer headed back from the Council meeting in Boise the minute they got wind of that brouhaha at the Compound gates. Too bad those are the last gates Cyrus got to see. I don't think the Pearly Gates will be opening for him." Magdalene's digression was unnerving.

"Mr. Darken? You said . . ."

"Oh, yes. What happened after they toted Cyrus off to cool with the sides of beef. Gomer dashed home lickity-split when he heard Marybeth yelling like a stuck pig in the front yard. That was after Maylene took the duct tape off her mouth," she chuckled.

"Your uncle is a fine-looking man. Like a pirate with that cutlass chopping through those blackberry vines. I watched him and those two men coming out through that rock wall behind my house. I had my telescope trained on that place and saw them taking your mother and sister back into the cave."

"What about Mr. Darken, Magdalene? You were going to tell me something." I tried to keep the frustration out of my voice.

"I am. I am. It relates. Your uncle had to tie Marybeth to a chair and put duct tape on that mouth of hers to get away with your mother and sister. Some time after they had gone, Maylene cut her free. I'd have given anything ..." She paused again.

"When Gomer got to the house, Marybeth told him the men that took Clara and Lorena had more than half an hour head start. She said Maylene hadn't cut her loose in time to send up an alert to stop those men. When Gomer asked her to explain, Maylene gave him a rhyme: 'They fled before night; serves you right.' That's when he punched her in the mouth—knocked out two teeth."

"And?" The narrative wasn't moving quickly enough for me.

"Maylene went into her room, packed everything she wanted in two pillowcases, and walked up the hill to my house. She wants to stay with me. Says she can drive me around. Says Gomer crossed the line." An odd babbling sound came through the phone—like one of those plastic whistle canaries that gurgle when you put water in them.

"I'm pleased as punch to have Maylene stay with me. I gave her an entire wing of the house and an old typewriter for doing her verse. I've already made an appointment with an endodontist in Boise. I'm treating us both to new teeth." She giggled.

"Gomer's been sitting in his pickup down at the bottom

of the hill this morning, but my hired men—they never could abide Cyrus—will keep him away. He's stuck with Marybeth for company. I reckon that's considerable punishment."

Her voice drifted into static. "Damn phone's temperamental. I'll get it fixed. I want to talk to my best friend often. Happy days ahead, my lovely Jenny."

THE SPLASHING OF brown pelicans diving into the water startled me. No sign of Uncle Hal's boat yet. Pip rose to a crouch and settled back again. Helen told me that some people consider pelicans symbols of Christ, believing that they feed their young with their own blood.

I told her that was nonsense; pelicans regurgitate food in their pouches for their young. She told me that her story was "prettier." Maybe.

Helen has traveled very far since we exited the tunnel from the Compound two months ago, but I don't think she can abandon what she believes. It might cost her too much emotionally.

We're the best of friends; sometimes I feel closer to Helen than to Mother. Then she throws in a zinger that opens my mouth like a hooked fish.

When we took the Liberty Head gold coins from her ancestor's crate in the cave to a Spokane jewelry store that deals with rare coins, she said: "We found these underground. Prophet Smith's tablets were also made of gold. He threw them back down the well into an ice-cold underground stream that flowed through chalcedony."

If there was a connection I didn't get it.

Neither did Aunt Izzy, nudging Helen in the back to agree to $32,000 for the coins. Nine of the coins were valued at around $2,000, but one minted in 1877 fetched $14,000.

As Aunt Izzy marched Helen to a local bank and helped her set up an account, Helen protested that the coins couldn't be worth such a sum. Then she said: "Just for Josh's college fund in case we don't settle things in the Compound."

During the past two months, some things have been slow to be settled in the Compound such as any official response to the property claims of Josh and his mother, although the Council moved with unusual speed to appoint Mr. Johnson, Abigail's father, as Elder to replace Elder Grund.

It gave me considerable pleasure to think of Gomer Darken brooding over that slight..

Other things have moved as fast as a neutrino. A case in point: Magdalene Marchman Grund. While words were being said over Cyrus Grund at the Zion Chapel with all the bigwigs from the Wards in attendance, Magdalene commandeered one of her hired men to drive her to Boise to visit the legal firm her father had used before his death.

Magdalene's property was in perfect order—everything in her name just as her father had intended. After her father's death, Cyrus had kept her a virtual prisoner in her own house and managed her property as though it were his. It wasn't.

Filing charges against a corpse proved difficult even for someone as determined as Magdalene. So, she petitioned for an annulment of her marriage, a reinstatement of her maiden name, and offered her sisterwife Griselda one of the worker's cottages until someone else could "claim" her.

Pumped up by Magdalene's spirit of independence,

Maylene jumped on her bandwagon. She didn't file for divorce or report Mr. Darken for bigamy, but she encouraged Mother to charge him with a Class C Felony in Oregon so he won't come across the state line.

I talk to Magdalene almost every day on the phone. Her money talks too. Her lawyer helped her buy a new fire engine red Mercedes. Maylene is teaching her to drive it.

We expect a visit from Magdalene within the month. I told Aunt Izzy that Magdalene is a fan of Henry James. She can hardly wait to meet her.

The boys are already in classes at the university in Eugene. Josh whizzed through CLEP tests as though not attending a high school wasn't an issue. He and Heath are sharing an apartment off campus.

"You can live with us when you start college, Jenny." Heath had assured me with a sly grin. "We'll share a room in a couple of years."

Sooner rather than later I wanted to tell Heath if I take advantage of CEEB and CLEP and the local community college to get college credits.

After months of missing school, I thought that I could never settle into the routine of normal class work again. Some days, I am totally disoriented, purposeless.

Continuing to miss my father but idolizing our elegant Euclid, I often feel more like the half-mad Pythagoras, clever at trigonometry but issuing edicts like his famous ones: "Don't ever eat beans" and "Do not eat your heart."

"Keep your thumb out of your mouth; drink eight glasses of water a day; do your multiplication tables," I remind Lorena like a scratched vinyl record that can't get past the damage and move on. Mother says I'm too bossy. She told me that Lorena needs to heal, just as we all do. Mother may be right.

Lorena no longer wets the bed. At the Johnson house, she had to hang her wet sheets on the clothesline outside. The cure was humiliation in front of the other children. Her response had been to refuse to drink water to the point of chronic dehydration.

Uncle Hal is good medicine for Lorena, but she sometimes thinks he might be our father, having risen as miraculously from the dead as Lazarus.

Lorena can put a Biblical twist on almost any situation or quote Shirley Temple *ad nauseam.*

Abigail's mother had a stash of VHS tapes of old Shirley Temple movies. Lorena's treat for learning a bible verse a day was a movie before bedtime. I just bought her an iPod and packed it with Taylor Swift. It may bring her around.

Economically, we've all come around. The proceeds from the diamond ring that Mr. Darken gave Mother (after it made the rounds with Maylene and Marybeth) pays the rent on a house next to Uncle Hal—and provided a new kiln for Helen—and her business associate, Mother.

Mother—a woman I sometimes would like to trade for Helen were it not for the incest issue with her son—surprised all of us. She dabs on pottery, splashing paint in bright, primary colors to create phantasmagorical sea creatures—a bit like Calder's drawings.

The back orders for her work are staggering. These days, she talks about her career more than shoes. I try not to talk about the future. I'm still sorting out the present.

My indebtedness to Magdalene troubles me. I've soaked and oiled the works and polished the outside of the Breguet watch I found in her ancestor's trunk in the cave. Helen says Magdalene will be overcome when she sees it. It seems a small thing to give her.

I sent all her deeds and papers to her lawyer in Boise. When I asked her where to send her rings, she snapped: "I thought I told you that they were yours—your college fund, Jenny." (She hadn't. She'd just sewed them around the scarf covering her great-grandfather's journals and handed them to me at our first meeting in the dark of the night.)

Magdalene was just as adamant about her will. "Everything goes to you and Josh. That's what I said, and that's what I mean. You can split it any way that you like when I'm gone. Move into this house if you want to." She giggled like a young girl.

Not any torture that Torquemada could dream up would take me back to the Compound. Helen has memories of a better time there. Even Josh speaks fondly of his childhood.

The bristly ear hairs of Gomer Darken and chicken legs of Jerry Winner spoiled every memory of that place—though I'd admit the scenery was magnificent.

AT THE FAR END of the dock, I could see Uncle Hal's boat heading toward his slip. Pip was on point. We'd have salmon or ling cod for dinner. Maybe even some of those scrumptious Dungeness crabs. Helen was great at gutting them. I couldn't seem to develop the aptitude.

I watched Uncle Hal and Helen walking hand-in-hand along the jetty. That was part of my malaise—not being able to figure out who belonged with whom.

From the moment I had spotted Uncle Hal with Lorena on his shoulders and Mother being supported by the Tomeh brothers on the bluff outside the cave, I knew that Uncle Hal had come to repair our family, to erase Gomer Darken's taint, to restore something of my father to me. He hadn't.

Mother, Helen, and Lorena moved into the small vacant house next to Uncle Hal; I opted to take the bedroom in his house that he had decorated just for me—before he had ever seen me—rather than share a room with Lorena.

We ate most of our meals together and listened to music at Uncle Hal's. The electricity in the room had nothing to do with the past relationship of my uncle and mother. That fuse had sputtered out long ago. He had eyes only for Helen Barnes.

At the far end of the jetty, I could see Lorena and Mother coming our way, making a zigzag pattern like sailors who hadn't found their sea legs. Lorena was doing that odd little skip, flashing her dimples, tossing her golden curls and impersonating Shirley as only she could do.

As I watched the flash of Lorena's ill-fitting, had-to-have ballerina flats smacking the boardwalk in a perfect rhythmic pattern, I fondly thought of the half-mad but fully sane Pythagoras who said: "There is geometry humming in the strings."

We didn't need to wait for "The Good Ship Lollipop." It had already docked.

THE END

THE LAND TRILOGY

Land of Nod

Land of the Bong Tree

Land of Lyonesse

Another novel by **Peggy Gardner**

A WINDING SHEET

The dark and twisted past of her ancestor, Octavius Wolfe, ensnares his only living descendant in a web of century-old murders as Isabella Wolfe, a young physician, returns to her ancestral home in Southern Oklahoma.

A Winding Sheet entangles Isabella in a past that will not be denied in spite of her self-imposed exile for fifteen years. Desperate to discover the link between recent deaths and the hundred-year-old bones of two young girls in her family cemetery, Isabella challenges an instrument of death that hangs by her own family tree.

A Winding Sheet takes Isabella into a sinister world where her great-great grandfather's dream of an empire threatens the life of his only living descendant.

What reviewers are saying about *A Winding Sheet:*

"I was hoping the story would never end, because it was so beautifully written, just like a song that you could listen to over and over again."

—E. F.

"A thoroughly enjoyable, superbly crafted book. An enthralling novel with an authentic sense of the stark atmosphere of Southern Oklahoma."

—G. H.

"Gardner's lush, evocative descriptions of the Oklahoma landscape are those of a writer lovingly familiar with her subject, her keen medical insight that of an observant insider. This masterfully crafted and detailed novel will have you on the edge of your seat."

—J. M.

Acknowledgments

Many thanks to my friends and relatives for their critiques and suggested improvements to *Land of Lyonesse*—and, especially to my colleagues at the Bandon Writers Group.

A special thank-you to Debbie O'Byrne for her exceptional cover designs.

About the Author

Peggy Gardner began her career as a journalist, taught English Literature, managed medical education, clinics and research for a major hospital, and has traveled extensively with her husband, daughter, and son. She currently resides in Oregon for the incomparable splendor of its coast.

www.ingramcontent.com/pod-product-compliance
Lightning Source LLC
Chambersburg PA
CBHW051505170626
46811CB00002B/660